"I want yourself to me."

Hassan held a lock of her hair as he spoke and was rubbing it sensuously between his finger and thumb. "I want your submission, Tiffany."

"No," she whispered.

How she hated him for what he was doing to her, she thought bitterly. He was making her come to terms with the fact that she wasn't cool and controlled at all, beneath the surface.

"There is one alternative," he said slowly.

"What would I have to do?" she asked in a chilly whisper, grasping at the straw of hope.

Hassan smiled hungrily, his lashes hiding the expression in his eyes as he said, "Become my wife."

SARA WOOD lives in a rambling sixteenth-century home in the medieval town of Lewes amid the Sussex hills. Her sons have claimed the cellar for bikes, making ferret cages, taxidermy and winemaking, while Sara has virtually taken over the study with her reference books, word processor and what have you. Her amiable, tolerant husband, she says, squeezes in wherever he finds room. After having tried many careers—secretary, guest house proprietor, play-group owner and primary teacher— she now finds writing romance novels gives her enormous pleasure.

Books by Sara Wood

SARA WOOD

desert hostage

Harlequin Books

TORONTO • NEW YORK • LONDON
AMSTERDAM • PARIS • SYDNEY • HAMBURG
STOCKHOLM • ATHENS • TOKYO • MILAN

Harlequin Presents first edition November 1991
ISBN 0-373-11414-1

Original hardcover edition published in 1990
by Mills & Boon Limited

DESERT HOSTAGE

CHAPTER ONE

TIFFANY almost dropped the armful of watered silk she had been carrying. Instead, she recovered her wits and placed it carefully on a table before turning slowly to face her partner.

'Cancelled?' Her voice sounded shaky. 'Palm Sands? Charlie, that's terrible! It's the second contract to be withdrawn! What's happening? Has the mafia invaded Oman?'

Charles was about to answer when their secretary buzzed on the intercom. The distracted Tiffany picked up the phone.

'There's a Sheikh Hassan here,' said an unusually breathless Leonie. 'Says he wants to discuss an important project.'

Tiffany and Charles exchanged glances. The man didn't have an appointment, but that wasn't unusual. And if he was a prospective customer...

'Please show the sheikh some of our portfolios,' said Tiffany. 'And say we'd be delighted to see him in five minutes.'

She replaced the receiver with a frown, staring through an arched window at the lapping waters of the Arabian Gulf below.

'Looks as if we have another paranoid sheikh who won't give his full name,' she sighed. 'More bulky body-guards, shouldering into our office with lumpy muscles and itchy trigger fingers.'

'Last one to spot the sheikh's bullet-proof vest and gun holster gets to pay for a round of drinks at the club,' Charles said with a grin.

'If the man has a palace here in Seeb which needs decorating, he can pack ten pistols and ride through that door on an Arab stallion for all I care,' said Tiffany drily. 'With the Palm Sands project a dead duck, we need a nice fat commission.'

Charles shook his head, bewildered. 'It's incredible how abruptly the contract was cancelled. Almost as if someone had heard we were crooks. You haven't anything in your past you're ashamed of, have you?'

'In twenty-six years? Plenty,' she sighed. 'Haven't we all? But nothing to explain why we've lost two juicy projects.'

'We'll find out the reason,' reassured Charles. 'In the meantime, let's roll out the red carpet, flash the teeth and gums nicely and impress the man like hell.'

'And for me, the cool, efficient look?' she grinned.

'Allow me.'

Laughing, Charles passed her the powder-blue jacket of her neatly waisted suit. As she slipped into it, there was a glint of silver out to sea. Her eyes focused on the glistening fish piled in a rope boat, hand-rolled from coconut husks. It was homeward bound for Muscat after an early morning fishing trip.

Home. For her it was anywhere she could get work. Maybe this time she and her eight-year-old son Josef could settle down. *If* Oriental Interiors could get enough contracts.

Hastily, she improved on her almost impeccable appearance, loosing her honey-blonde hair and deftly twisting it back with graceful movements into a severely pinned knot.

The situation was worrying. After six months, she and Charlie had almost finished their work on the hotel where they had temporary offices. And there was nothing else on the horizon, now the two major contracts for the year had been cancelled. The financial compensation wouldn't be enough to cover their expenses. And if there was some kind of vendetta against them, they were in trouble. Reputation out here was everything.

'Ready?'

She composed herself. A perfect English rose, reserved, controlled, and very unapproachable. A lady. Prim and proper.

She nodded, just as Leonie knocked and slipped into the office, looking very agitated.

'He's getting impatient,' she said, upset. 'He's walking up and down and looking angrier and angrier. His eyes are lethal. Can I tell him you're almost ready?'

'Show him in, Leonie,' said Charles. He raised an eyebrow at Tiffany. 'We have an arrogant man on our hands, it seems.'

'I'll try to remember we're on the breadline and the creditors are knocking on the door,' she said grimly. She didn't like bombastic, self-important men. They reminded her of her late husband, Nazim.

The nervous Leonie showed the Arab into the exotic, mirrored room, rich in oriental golds and reds, in gilt and marble.

Tiffany's grey eyes widened. Sheikh Hassan stood out, even in his ostentatious surroundings. Running a designer's expert eyes over him, she assessed the cost of the handmade Italian suit. It had been built on him, and an excellent construction job it was too. He must have had dozens of fittings for the suit to have fitted so smoothly over that hard, fit body.

Her lips curved into a faint smile. The lines were so clean and sharp that no weaponry—other than his undoubtable male virility—could possibly be hidden beneath the soft grey cloth.

He had paused, blocking the doorway, an effective and commanding entrance. Charles was walking towards him, his hand outstretched, but the sheikh stood solid and immovable, only his dark lustrous eyes scanning the room, no smile on his harsh face.

Then he came forward, startling Tiffany with the swiftness of his sudden, energetic stride and directness of his gaze on Charles.

'Sheikh Hassan. How do you do?' said Charles warmly. 'I am Charles Porter, the head designer of Oriental Interiors.'

'How do you do?' murmured the sheikh. The bright sun, filtering through the stone tracery of the windows, gleamed richly on his glossy blue-black hair.

He left Charles and swung around to Tiffany, moving with that sudden, unharnessed speed which betrayed a fierce vitality. She had an impression of a man who was more used to vigorous gallops across the desert than moving within the confines of a room.

'I am Tiffany Sharif,' she offered, with a cool smile. 'Mr Porter's partner and assistant designer.'

He caught her elegant, artistic hand in a grip of hard iron which drew her off balance and made her stumble closer to him. An angry light flashed briefly in her eyes. Astonishingly, she had recognised that he had fully intended to make her do that. A nasty piece of one-upmanship.

She stared down at the long, tanned fingers impassively.

He didn't let her go. He was crowding her space, his chest rising and falling in a powerful and daunting swell, only a short distance from the plush fullness of her jutting breasts, and she didn't like being that close to any man, let alone this one.

He disconcerted her with his vibrant energy, a lust for living, which made him immediately overbearing.

Keep your distance, her expression said boldly.

He ignored the message. 'I am Sheikh Hassan. Delighted. Absolutely delighted,' he said tightly.

Tiffany's eyes narrowed. There was something oddly sinister about the way he said that. A veiled threat. A sense of unease settled over her.

'What a strong handshake,' she remarked pointedly, injecting a little frost into her voice and expecting he would release her. He didn't.

'I tame horses,' he said cynically. 'High-spirited ones. You need strength to overcome wayward animals and show them who is their master.'

She reeled inwardly from the meaning behind his words. He was trying to dominate her and, dammit, she wasn't in any position to give him any backchat!

'How thrilling!' she fluttered, taking the only way out.

He wasn't fooled. He was too smart.

'Even more thrilling when the training is over and a mere movement of my body brings instant obedience,' he said with soft menace.

Secretly fuming, Tiffany nodded, apparently wide-eyed with admiration. She'd jerk him out of his complacency. Far too many men played macho games with her. She fixed a fascinated smile to her cold face. 'You're the second jockey I've met. The last one was banned for using his whip.'

The Arab's chest inflated dangerously and his hand slid from hers. Tiffany was forced to drop her lashes, intimidated by his anger, for a wave of cold, remembered fear had washed through her, bringing a terrible memory of violence to the surface. And she hated the sheikh for reminding her of that.

'Please, do sit down,' said Charles hastily. 'Have you had a long journey?'

The sheikh moved to the gold damask ottoman. 'New York. This morning.'

Tiffany looked at him with grudging respect. He appeared to be as fresh as a daisy. Into the hothouse atmosphere of the office, his clear, desert-hawk eyes and healthily glowing face had brought an air of the outdoors—a harsh, arid and merciless landscape, set under a cruel sun.

'May we offer you some refreshment?' she asked politely. 'Perhaps coffee? Or a soft drink?'

'A large neat whisky, if you have it.'

Tiffany blinked, but went to the cupboard where alcohol was kept discreetly for European visitors. Ten o'clock in the morning and he was on the bottle!

'Jet lag,' explained the sheikh, his mocking eyes watching Tiffany walk smoothly back across the room towards him. 'My body tells me it's late evening and is making its usual demands.'

She was holding the glass out to him and trying to keep her face blank, but from the way his voice caressed the words, and his roving glance had crawled up her long, long dancer's legs, he was obviously making a point about more than his drinking habits.

What an unpleasant man.

'Where would you like your drink?' she asked with a nearly sweet smile, as if contemplating a few interesting places.

He grinned, the flash of his white teeth dazzling in his tanned face. Smoke-grey eyes met ebony and locked. The grin faded. Something utterly unexpected in his expression caught her attention and held it, preventing her from looking away.

It was dislike! No, more than that, she corrected; it was a scathing contempt, which spoiled his handsome face, curling his smooth upper lip and tightening the muscles of his beautifully carved jaw!

'On the table.'

Her mouth pursed at the arrogant order, but she controlled her temper and flashed him a beaming smile.

Charles began to make conversation. Tiffany walked to her chair and sat down, every movement graceful, every gesture harmonious. Her poise was as natural as breathing.

Adoring ballet as a child, she'd been pushed too hard by an ambitious mother and at the age of sixteen had struggled on in pain, her ankles weakened by overwork. Her promising career was finished and she had a feeling of guilt that her mother's financial sacrifices had been in vain.

Her subsequent oriental-design course, however brief it had been before her marriage to Nazim, had proved useful. When he had died in London, she and little Josef had faced poverty until she'd applied for a job with Charles. He didn't mind that she'd never finished her design course because he liked her ideas, her flair and the polished presentation—evidence of hard work. They'd hit it off immediately, and Tiffany had happily followed him when he'd decided to look for work in Oman. She and Josef had travelled enough in their lives not to mind a move to the Middle East.

She listened to the two men chatting and wisely kept her mouth shut. The sheikh seemed happy now he was talking to Charles. It was plain that he was a raving chauvinist and she'd better keep in the background for the sake of the project.

'...a leisure complex, for weary businessmen,' the
sheikh was saying. 'On the Batinah coast, here in Oman.
I've financed it. As well as the usual facilities, it houses
an ice rink, golf course, clubhouse, swimming-pools,
health club, fishing wharfs...'

Tiffany's head reeled as he rattled through the list.
What with the public rooms, secretarial areas, offices
and restaurants, their work would be cut out to master-
mind a coherent design. It was the chance of a lifetime.
Her eyes became brilliant with hope and her face lit up
with excitement.

'Sharif, you said?'

She started at the venom in his tone, directed at her.
He glanced at her left hand, which bore no wedding-
ring. She'd removed it the day Nazim had died and never
wanted to wear one again. And then his glittering,
diamond-hard eyes flicked up to hers again and stayed
there.

Didn't he have eyelashes, and blink, like the rest of
humanity? she wondered, a little shaken. It was like being
hypnotised by a bird of prey! His open scorn reminded
her of Nazim. The translucent skin over her cheekbones
stretched taut with strain.

'Correct,' she said stiffly.

'Not an English name. And yet I can't believe that
you have hot Arab blood racing beneath that pale, soft
skin.'

He sat there in a very self-contained way, one long leg
crossed elegantly over the other, his pure white shirt
cutting a sharply defined line against his dark throat.
One tanned hand rested on his silver-grey-clad thigh, the
other on the rich damask seat. Everywhere on his person
there was the glint of gold; on his wrist, in the deep-shot
cuffs, on his little finger, and making a neat bar across
his grey tie.

And oh, yes, he had eyelashes—long, curling and thick, briefly hooding his eyes as he watched her absorbing all this detail, an imperceptible quirk now shaping the masculine, and disturbingly sensual lines of his mouth. Apart from these slight movements, only the gentle swell of his chest betrayed the pulsing life within him.

'How right you are, Sheikh Hassan. I'm pure English, through and through. Pure as the driven snow,' she said coolly. That should tell him where he stood!

'Then I assume you married an Omani.' An unpleasant smile briefly touched his lips. 'The cold, fair beauty has fallen in love with the darkness of the sultry night.'

Darkness was right, she thought with a wince. The darkness of hell. How romantic he made her ghastly marriage sound.

Her hand had involuntarily touched her breast, unwittingly drawing the sheikh's attention to her swelling curves. She saw that his dark, penetrating eyes had become as warm and inviting as hot caramel. Inwardly recoiling, Tiffany recognised the signs of danger in his regard. If he was to see her as anything other than a woman designed for man's pleasure, she'd need to freeze him down. She iced her eyes over till they were as dark as gun-metal.

'I married an Arab,' she said in a low voice.

'Do you have a family, Sheikh Hassan?' asked Charles awkwardly, seeing that Tiffany was becoming distressed.

'No one close. Though soon there will be,' he answered. 'Your husband——'

'Sir...' Charles bit his lip, but was emboldened by Tiffany's white, strained face. 'Forgive me for interrupting, but Mrs Sharif prefers not to speak of her late husband. Nazim died tragically in a car crash, two years ago.'

The effect on Sheikh Hassan was extraordinary. It was as if he had drawn back into himself, despite the fact that not one muscle of his body had visibly moved.

'How very sad. I trust you are not entirely alone. Your parents must have been a great comfort to you.'

Tiffany frowned at his silky intrusion into her private life.

'I never knew my father. Mother died last year,' she said shortly.

'You have sons, Mrs Sharif?' he asked softly.

For some inexplicable reason, she sensed danger in his question. Yet it was a polite query, one which might well be asked in such circumstances. She knew that in the Arab world a son would grow up to provide for his widowed mother, whereas a daughter would be a financial burden until her bride price had been paid.

'One son. He is all the family I have.'

Sweet Josef. Without her knowing, her face grew tender, its beauty breathtaking as she mentally contemplated her handsome, beloved son.

'And yet you work,' murmured the sheikh.

'For his sake, I must,' she answered, with a tilt of her chin at the implied criticism. 'Josef is a day boy at Gulf International, the boarding school in Muscat. My hours are arranged so that I am home when he returns.'

The sheikh's disapproval had deepened, now he knew she was a working mother. Tiffany felt her stomach twist. The chance of winning this marvellous contract was slipping away. All because she was a woman, and she wasn't at home washing clothes and doing the ironing.

'Mrs Sharif doesn't allow her domestic life to interfere with her work. You can be sure that we both devote ourselves to our assignments,' said Charles, misinterpreting the reason for the sheikh's stony face. 'You only have to look around you to see that we must have put in some considerable thought and time to working on this hotel. The style...' he flicked open a folder and handed it to the sheikh '...is traditional, using the best of Oman's historical designs.'

They waited in silence while Sheikh Hassan examined the portfolio carefully, his face brooding.

'I'll have a contract drawn up this afternoon. That is, if you want the work,' he said abruptly.

'Oh! We would prefer to offer you some preliminary designs first——' began Charles, astonished at the speed of the sheikh's decision. Out here, even the smallest decisions normally took weeks, even months.

'I can see the quality of your work. I already knew of it, anyway. I was involved in the Palm Sands project.' Hassan's eyes flicked to and from Charles and Tiffany, gauging their reactions. He smiled to himself at their evident surprise. 'I know a great deal about you both. We'll get down to details later.' He stood up in a beautifully flowing movement. Harmony, thought Tiffany in surprise. The man moved with grace. 'How fortunate I am that you are free to concentrate on my leisure centre.'

He looked at Tiffany. And so sudden was the turning on of his sexuality that it poured unhindered into her senses, blocking everything else, like a powerful electric shock. A harsh, uncompromising desire flickered in his face, arching the strong mouth into sultry curves, parting his lips over the white teeth.

'And how fortunate I am to have met you, Mrs Sharif. I will be...' he considered carefully, his eyes hotly inciting '...as you say...*in touch*.'

With those softly growled words, he nodded, and strode out before either Charles or Tiffany could respond.

She was trying to cope with the unsettling fact that his deep, rich voice still seemed to be vibrating through her whole body. She'd never known a man so steeped in sexuality that it had the power to hit her in a forceful wave. He'd deliberately let her glimpse the blatant, raw carnality behind his temporary mask of a sophisticated businessman. A flash of intuition told her that beneath the western dress lay a man in tune with a far more primitive life than she could imagine—one which was stripped of everything but the bare essentials for survival: water, food, sex.

The perfectly tailored clothes and cultured voice had vividly contrasted with the almost indecent passion for life in that tautly honed body. Everything about him added up to the enviable, self-confident air of a man who had mastered the art of living in a hard and remorseless environment. And the fact that he was able to successfully step from the harshness of a barren desert straight into an urban jungle was an even more unnerving achievement.

'Whew!' Charles drew a stubby-fingered hand over his forehead. 'Some dynamite!'

'One of the most unpleasantly pushy men I've ever met,' muttered Tiffany. 'Oh, don't worry, Charlie. I can work for swine like him if I have to. That work will keep us in coffee-beans and doughnuts for years. We have to sign. And somehow, I get the feeling that he's tied up with those cancellations. He knew too much about Palm Sands for my liking.'

'We'll push on and finish our work here, then,' said Charles. 'And see what Sheikh Hassan has to offer. I think,' he said, his face blissfully happy, 'that we've just met the goose who goes about laying golden eggs!'

Tiffany smiled faintly. She wasn't so sure. There was something underhand and sinister about the sheikh. And he was no goose. More a savage and hungry wolf.

At the end of the day, she walked through the crowded souk to her tiny flat, situated above a tailor's shop. It was all she'd been able to afford. Nazim's creditors had taken everything and she was still paying off a massive overdraft.

Then there were Josef's school fees. For him, she'd make any sacrifice. He'd have the best education she could buy. Turning down a narrow alley, only as wide as a camel's haunches, she stared up at the flaking old building where she lived. A grimace crossed her face. It was shabby, but they had no choice for the moment, and at least their neighbours were decent people.

Greeting the friendly tailor, she went slowly up the worn steps to her flat. Half an hour later, Josef was dropped off by the school bus and came bursting in, full of news about his day.

By eight o'clock they had eaten. Josef had changed into some old clothes and gone to his room to do some homework. Tiffany had showered, and washed her hair, leaving it to hang down her back to dry naturally. Slipping on a silk kimono, she sat in her bedroom doing her nails by the fading light from the window. There was a knock on the sitting-room door, and her hand holding the nail-polish brush wobbled a little.

'Who is it?' she called loudly, concentrating on smoothly lacquering her nails. Appearance was very important in her job.

'It's me.'

'Come in, Mike. Come through to the bedroom.' She looked up and smiled at her friend, the serious young newly-wed from the room below. 'Hello. How's Mandy?'

Mike's homely face softened and Tiffany felt a pang to see the love he felt for Mandy. She envied the couple.

'Lovely, as always,' he said happily. 'How can you do that in the dark?'

'I hadn't noticed it was,' she said. 'Can you put the light on for me, Mike? My nails are wet.'

'Sure. I came to ask if you need anything in Muscat. I'm going there tomorrow.'

Tiffany flicked back a lock of hair from her eyes and blinked when an eyelash entered her eye.

'Damn.' She tried to remove it with her knuckle, not wanting to spoil her nails.

'Shall I help?' offered Mike tentatively, after watching her struggle for a few seconds.

'Please. It's really painful.'

She tipped up her face to his and he knelt in front of her, his face screwed up in concentration as he brushed at her lid with his clean handkerchief.

'Thanks,' she said gratefully. 'Um...Muscat. No, I don't think we want anything—but it was nice of you to ask.'

'OK. Call in or leave a note if you change your mind,' he said.

They talked for a few moments about Jo, then he said goodbye, shutting her bedroom door as he went.

Soon after, she heard another rap on the outer door, loud enough to be heard in the bedroom. She hoped Jo would answer it this time. It was bound to be one of his friends. They called often, not seeming to mind what the place looked like. He was very popular. Soon he'd want to board at the school as they did; in fact, he'd pestered her for ages, till she'd had to tell him she couldn't yet afford the extra fees. But she knew she would have to be prepared to watch her son become more and more independent.

Jo needed the balance of a male world, as well as a female one. She'd noticed how much he loved hearing from his friends about the activities they enjoyed with their fathers. It hurt her a little that she couldn't be everything to him. She grinned to herself. Her skills as a footballer left much to be desired!

From the sitting-room came a man's voice, and Josef's delighted laughter. It must be Mike again.

As she approached the connecting door, with a gentle smile on her face, she could hear Josef speaking, his voice high with excitement.

'... and I'm in the rugby team, too. Shall I get Mum? She'll be knocked sideways when she knows who you are! Isn't it brilliant?'

She stopped in surprise. That wasn't like her reserved, thoughtful son! A deep, warm chuckle echoed through the small lounge. Tiffany didn't recognise that as Mike's. But she did recognise the voice which spoke afterwards. Only one man could project pagan sensuality through solid chipboard.

Sheikh Hassan. A chill spread down Tiffany's spine. How on earth had he discovered her address? And why? Her lips firmed into a straight and determined line. She'd known there was more to the arrogant sheikh than met the eye. What tale was he spinning to her son?

Pushing open the door quietly, she saw him sitting on her dilapidated sofa, dressed for an expensive night out in an immaculate dinner-jacket and looking out of place in the down-at-heel room. His arm lay affectionately around Josef. Neither of them looked up.

To her horrified eyes, the two of them were totally wrapped up in each other, beaming stupidly, their eyes shining as if they'd won a lottery. Tiffany was more shocked than she could have imagined.

'Sheikh Hassan! What, *precisely*, are you doing with my son?' she rapped out, her face hot with fury.

Hassan was caught off guard. His eyes momentarily showed the traces of warmth he had been sharing with Josef, and then a brief flash of fierce, sexual approval as his glance flashed over Tiffany's flowing hair and the revealing robe which rose and fell with every angry breath she took. Then the shutters came down over his face again, and by that time she was coping with Josef, who had flung himself into her arms.

'It's all right, Mum!' he cried, hugging her with all his might.

He looked at her as if he was dizzy with happiness, and her heart lurched. She reached out a tender hand and stroked his dark wavy hair, a feeling of foreboding in every one of her bones.

'Darling,' she reproved sternly, 'this...person is——'

'You don't know, you don't know who he is *really*!' crowed Josef, laughing.

He ran to Hassan, who had risen, and in a swift eager movement the sheikh caught him up, bubbling with suppressed laughter, and held him close as if they'd known each other for a loving lifetime. Tiffany's heart did another little somersault to see the sheikh's tenderness and she clutched at the door-frame in confusion. This was extraordinary behaviour for Josef! He was deeply loving, but like her he saved his affection for those he knew well. A terrible chill sent icicles into her stomach.

'Who are you?' she snapped, intensely irritated at the bond which seemed to have been so easily cemented between the uninvited sheikh and her son.

'My uncle! My very own uncle!' said Josef with a blissful smile, patently unable to tear his eyes away from the sheikh. 'Father's brother! Isn't it wonderful?'

Stunned, Tiffany was unable to speak. The breath had left her body in a sharp gasp. Her eyes and mouth shaped into circles. It was impossible! Nazim had sworn he was alone in the world. Why on earth would he lie?

She flicked back her long curtain of golden hair which had swung around her face, and tried to compose herself.

'Mum, it's true, it's true!' cried Josef, seeing her disbelief. 'And we're invited to Riyam! I can't wait to go! Uncle has told me all about my ancestors and the desert and the stables and the fortress and——'

'Just a minute, Josef,' Tiffany said weakly, her mind in turmoil.

'Sit down,' ordered Hassan, watching her like a hawk.

Too flabbergasted to demur, she obeyed, sinking limply into a chair, her long slender legs shaking. She didn't understand. He must have known who she was when he met her at the office. And then, his hatred of her had poured from his body in a never-ending stream.

Tiffany flushed. He'd deliberately given her the once-over. The leisure centre was a ruse, after all. Her future was still uncertain. A lead weight descended on her shoulders.

But... wasn't it a little suspicious that suddenly he'd come up with this story that they were related? It was all too far-fetched. He would have mentioned it before, surely?

'How can you possibly be my brother-in-law?' she said coldly.

'Oh, the usual way,' he drawled, arching a wicked eyebrow.

She flushed and he gave a mocking smile, reaching inside his dinner-jacket. He handed her his passport, which she took with trembling hands and an ominous feeling. If she did have a brother-in-law, she thought bleakly, she didn't want him to be this sardonic man whose every thought seemed to be laced with sexual violence. She shuddered. That alone linked him to Nazim.

With trembling fingers, she opened up the leather folder and flicked over the pages. Hassan bin Hamud al Sharif. Age thirty-two. Born in Riyam, in the city of Shirbat. The same place as her late husband Nazim. She raised her head and met Hassan's dangerous, black-ice eyes. What she saw there made the muscles in her stomach clench. Whatever he was up to, it was more sinister than she knew.

'He never mentioned you,' she breathed. 'He said he was alone in the world.'

'He was, in a way. There'd been a family row. Nazim left Riyam fifteen years ago, when he was twenty,' said Hassan quietly, keeping his arm tightly around Josef, who was gazing at him adoringly.

'Do you play football?' asked Jo hopefully.

'Do I?' grinned the sheikh. 'You try me!'

'Rugby? Cricket?'

'Yes. You like sport?'

Jo hugged himself in delight. 'You bet! But I don't ride.'

'You will,' promised Sheikh Hassan, testing Josef's muscles, and lifting one eyebrow. 'I think you're even stronger than I was at your age,' he said in surprise.

Josef fell for that flattery, to Tiffany's tight-lipped annoyance.

'Wow! Does that mean I'll grow up to be as big as you?' he asked, betraying his hero-worship by his expression.

Oh, God! thought Tiffany, a chill in her spine. Josef has found the father he's always longed for!

'Sheikh Hassan,' she said sharply, 'I went through Nazim's papers. There was nothing about any family— no photographs, no letters——'

'My father disowned him. I suppose he destroyed everything to do with us. In fact, we heard nothing from him till he contacted us a few years ago, shortly before my father died. Nazim was in Turkey...' Hassan hesitated, flicking a glance at Josef as if quickly altering what he had intended to say. 'He wrote to tell me there were some difficulties with the authorities,' he finished tactfully. 'He knew Father would never assist him, so I helped him out.'

Tiffany's grey eyes darkened in pain. Difficulties! That was putting it mildly. Until this day, she'd never known how Nazim had escaped a prison sentence for smuggling Persian carpets, nor how they'd all managed to slip out of the country and find the means to return to England.

'You sent money,' she said flatly.

'Yes. And pulled strings.' His eyes bore remorselessly into hers. 'And started him up in business again.'

'*You?* Oh, my God! I see!'

She frowned. So she was in Hassan's debt! The thought was too ghastly to imagine. Perhaps he'd come to demand payment, and the interest. A small groan escaped her lips.

'That doesn't prove you're Nazim's brother,' she said, putting off the evil moment when she might have to accept that fact. 'Just because you lent him money and your name is Sharif. It's not an uncommon name, is it?'

'I have documentary proof which will confirm that I am. I will show you it. We will have dinner together. There is a great deal to discuss,' said Hassan in a low tone.

Josef's face fell and he sullenly fiddled with his threadbare cuff, his mouth pouting his disappointment.

'You can't go out without me! We've only just met! I want to ask you——'

A brief gesture of Hassan's firm hand stopped Josef's protest immediately. Tiffany was rather surprised. Her son could be very strong-willed when he wanted to be.

'Josef,' said Hassan, in a voice of infinite gentleness, 'I understand what you feel. I, too, am loath to leave you. But I must talk to your mother urgently. Be patient. We'll have years together. I told you I must return to Riyam late tonight. You can see I have to quickly convince your mother that I am your uncle.'

Hassan accepted Josef's bright-eyed nod. Tiffany was utterly astonished that her son seemed on the edge of tears. What had Hassan told him when they were alone? He must have played on her son's need for a father, as she'd thought. And what dreams of luxury had he coaxed Josef with?

'Why didn't you say anything when we first met?' she asked, in an accusing tone.

'I wasn't absolutely sure you were the right woman. Then, when you confirmed it with one or two remarks, I thought you'd rather hear the news in the privacy of your own home.'

His disdainful glance swept around the tiny room, leaving her in no doubt as to his opinion of it.

'I can't have dinner with you,' she said coldly. 'Josef——'

'Wouldn't Mike and Mandy keep an ear open for me?' begged Josef. 'I do want you to go, Mum! I do want you to believe Uncle Hassan! Besides,' he added craftily, 'you haven't been out since that man——'

'Jo,' she said hurriedly, not wanting to remember one of her less successful dates, a year ago. She'd come home feeling as if she'd been fending off a monster with eight pairs of hands.

'Why not go and ask these friends of yours?' suggested Hassan to Josef.

He leapt up. 'All right, Mum?'

'I have the contract here,' said Hassan quietly, patting his pocket. 'You could look at the terms over dinner and then we can talk about one or two things.'

'You're serious about the Batinah project?' she frowned, wavering.

She needed it so badly! Perhaps she could forget how much she disliked this man, and look on him as a bag of gold. She remembered Charlie's remark and smiled, correcting that to a golden egg.

'Go, Josef,' said Hassan. 'It'll do your mother good to go out.'

With Jo gone eagerly to do Hassan's bidding, the room seemed to shrink. She felt quite unnerved being alone with Hassan—and that was strange, since he was supposed to be her brother-in-law. The silence grew, and with it the atmosphere became oppressively heavy.

'You've dropped something of a bombshell on us,' she said eventually, desperate to break the tension.

'Josef seems thrilled. But not you,' drawled Hassan, lifting one dark eyebrow at an angle.

'You can hardly blame me for being cautious.'

He undid the button on his jacket and treated her to a broad expanse of dazzling white-shirted chest.

'Your son is puzzled and a little unhappy that you don't want him to have an uncle. It's almost as if you're jealous,' he murmured.

She flushed. 'I don't like strangers being familiar with my son,' she said stiffly. 'He knows that.'

'But...when you know for sure that I am your brother-in-law. Will I then be permitted to love Josef?'

Tiffany's face became troubled. As she contemplated the sheikh, her mouth parted, and she became aware of his eyes riveted to it. A small, sharp stab slid unwanted through her breast and her hand fluttered there, as if to keep it from troubling her again.

'You must understand,' she said, struggling with her wayward body and trying to keep her head. The sheikh had a remarkable ability to disconcert her—especially by using her own unfulfilled passions. He was drawing them out of her, like a master. 'The past is painful for me. Links with my late husband are naturally going to affect my equilibrium. You will have to be patient.'

'I have patience when I can see the result is worth waiting for,' he murmured, scalding her with an avid glance. 'I'll wait while you put some clothes on.'

To her amazement, she felt the heat of a sensual flame lick treacherously within her in response to his hot admiration. Confused by it, she wrapped her kimono securely around her body, then realised with a flush of embarrassment that she had pulled it taut over her breasts. Under the liquid darkness of his eyes, she folded her arms defiantly across her body, determined to resist him in every way.

'I don't think I want to go——'

'You have no choice,' he interrupted grimly, all gentleness gone. 'Oriental Interiors is in financial trouble. I can alleviate that pressure. People are beginning to talk about the mysterious cancelling of agreements. You know how important word of mouth is out here. Your good name is in my hands. I could make or break you and Charles Porter.'

She glared at his blatant blackmail.

'You wouldn't!'

'I would,' he said with soft menace.

'You threaten me——!'

'I have little time and I need to talk to you tonight,' he said impatiently. 'I'll use any means I have to. Do you really wish to disappoint your son? Can you dare to leave this matter unsettled? It's his future you're playing with, as well as your own, by disregarding my wishes.'

She stifled a sharp reply at his high-handed behaviour. Whether she liked it or not, he was right; she had to clear all this up, and not within Josef's earshot. But only if the stakes were high enough. If she was going to spend a couple of hours in his company, there might as well be something worthwhile coming from this ridiculous situation.

'Are you serious about the leisure complex?' she asked with a tilt of her firm chin as Jo hurtled back into the room.

Hassan smiled at the boy's excited face and embraced him fondly. Jo clung to him as if he never wanted him to go.

'Oh, yes,' he said, his eyes meeting Tiffany's over Josef's head. 'More than ever. I would like to keep my business in the family, and so I see no reason why we shouldn't sign the preliminary contract tonight if you are willing. The work is yours for the taking.'

Tiffany felt stunned. Josef bounced up and down on the sofa in glee.

'You see,' he grinned. 'You don't have to worry about money any more and working all hours! Uncle Hassan will take care of us! You needn't keep going to sales for clothes and walk miles for cheap vegetables. We can have meat a bit more often. You needn't worry about the rent and my school fees and my uniform. You——'

'Josef!' she breathed. 'Please!'

Hassan's face had turned to stone, his high cheekbones jutting aggressively beneath his glittering eyes. Tiffany could see that his anger was only barely held in check.

And the hatred had returned, blazing its destructive path through the air, slicing the atmosphere like a knife as they both matched each other, stare for stare.

So. That was the reason for his dislike of working mothers. In fact, it made his claim to kinship more probable; her brother-in-law thought that the women of his family should stay at home and be domesticated, devoting themselves entirely to their children. Everything began to fall into place: Hassan's anger when he arrived—he would have had an inkling that she was a career woman—and his searching questions.

Yet...there was a number of loose ends still. She frowned.

'Mother,' cried Josef, torn between the two of them, his face crumpled in anguish.

'Oh, Jo! It's all right,' she said quietly, holding out her arms and giving him a hug. 'Sheikh Hassan is right. Try to contain your excitement till the morning, and I'll get you up early so we can talk before school. You do want me to go, don't you?' she asked.

'Oh, yes, Mum!' he said earnestly.

'I'll get ready.' She hesitated, not wanting to leave them together.

'I won't harm him,' said Hassan with a cynical glance. 'These walls are so thin, I'm sure you'll be able to hear everything we say.'

She flushed. 'I won't be long,' she muttered. 'Jo, perhaps you'd like to get Sheikh Hassan a coffee. We don't have any whisky,' she said sharply.

'*Uncle* Hassan; he's my uncle,' corrected Josef.

'Your mother must make sure, for your sake,' said Hassan gently. 'She's a little reluctant to believe it. We have to win her round.'

Tiffany pursed her lips at this clever move to make it seem as if he and Josef were on the same side and she was the enemy. Unable to say what she wanted to, she whirled out. To her ears came the sound of much laughter. Uncle Hassan was turning out to be a stand-up comedian, she thought sourly.

Feeling very reluctant, Tiffany dragged on the only smart dress she had which wouldn't let the side down: a bright red, and rather gorgeous hip-hugging, scoop-necked sheath which Nazim had bought for her in one of his extravagant moods. She smoothed on a little eye make-up and lipstick and gave her hair a quick brush, wishing she dared take time to put it up. That would take too long, and she didn't like the cosy intimacy into which her son and the imperious stranger had fallen. The silence and low murmuring behind the door were even worse than the laughter.

She slipped on her high-heeled sandals and dragged on a light cotton jacket before taking a few deep breaths to compose herself.

Only outwardly, though. Her mind was still racing, still going over and over the claims the sheikh had made, and what their implications might be. It was no use wondering. She'd soon know. And the sooner she entered that room and actually got the man alone, the sooner she'd be able to speak frankly and find out what he was up to.

In trepidation, knowing this evening could make or break her and her son, Tiffany pushed open the door.

CHAPTER TWO

JOSEF was curled up with Hassan, looking sleepy, and it seemed that the sheikh was telling him a story.

A fairy-story, thought Tiffany uncharitably, listening to the soothing, hypnotic voice. Hassan was oblivious to everything but Josef.

'They call it Tawi Atair,' he was saying, almost dreamily.

'Tawi Atair,' repeated Josef drowsily. 'What does that mean, Uncle?'

'The well of birds. There are so many. Some you may never have seen before, and a few familiar friends. But you'll see for yourself. Soon. I can hardly wait for that day, Josef.'

'We must make sure there's no mistake, first,' said Tiffany sharply, feeling like a wet blanket when she saw her son's look of alarm and misery at the thought that she might prevent him from acquiring this adored uncle.

As for Hassan, he'd glanced up at her and his rogue's eyes were all but stripping her naked. She gave him a scathing glance.

'There's no mistake,' said Hassan, unperturbed, turning from her to smile at Josef with affection. 'Don't worry. Rely on me.'

Tiffany felt a stab within her chest at the love he seemed to be offering her son. Hassan seemed charged with a greater passion than most men built up in a lifetime. In fact, she had the impression that he was a bigger man in all ways than any male she'd ever known.

A natural born leader. Someone who'd stand out in any crowd.

She admired that. It had been her misfortune that Nazim had turned out to be weak-willed beneath his bluster, and had needed to enforce his male domination over her by crushing her spirit. She found the sheikh's inner strength rather refreshing, after that. Odd, if they were brothers.

'You look nice, Mum,' said Jo, his eyes pleading with her to like Hassan.

'Thank you, darling. Are you going downstairs to watch television with Mike?' she asked softly. For his sake, she'd sort this out. Josef nodded, beaming with pleasure.

Hassan stood up and reached out for Jo, picking him up in his strong arms. Tiffany was annoyed. It had been ages since she'd treated Jo like a baby; this man had no right to do so. It irked her even more that Jo seemed to be enjoying the temporary reversion to childhood, rather than being the sensible young boy, longing to be grown up.

By the time they left, she was very irritable. The sheikh had charmed everyone effortlessly, though he'd eyed Mike up and down a bit, as if he was a challenge.

The evening out started badly. They walked through the bustling streets to the square, which appeared to be filled with the biggest car she'd ever seen: a stretch limo, customised to please the most jaded of customers. She held on tight to her familiar portfolio, which Hassan had insisted she brought, and made her way through a small crowd which had collected around the gleaming car in awe.

Flushing with embarrassment at the ostentatious car, she stayed silent while Hassan ordered everyone out of the way and handed her in. It even smelt of money, she thought sourly—a strong aroma of soft leather. Inside, it was pretending to be a nuclear power station, with flashing lights, rows of dials and video screens.

The chauffeur drove off to a chorus of acclaim, as the car raised itself on its hydraulics and smoothly cruised away, like a huge vulture launching itself from a tree.

'It's not mine,' said Hassan tightly, seeing her disapproval. 'It belongs to a friend.'

'Amazing what bad taste some influential men have,' she said coldly, throwing caution to the winds and abandoning any idea of politeness.

'He's certainly influential,' murmured Hassan meaningfully.

'And he's certainly undiscerning,' she snapped.

'No, practical,' muttered Hassan. 'He needs a travelling office.'

He gestured to the computer and fax machine, and the two telephones.

'I'm surprised he can bear to lend the car to you,' she observed tartly. 'He'll get withdrawal symptoms, trying to manage without it tonight.'

'He's dining with the Sultan,' said Hassan in a flat voice.

'I'm staggered you weren't asked too,' she retorted.

'I was.'

He gave her a mocking smile. He was lying, of course. She half turned her back on him. It was an invidious situation, being in this man's debt, and thus in his power. Since the years with Nazim, when she'd been helplessly trapped by his threats, she'd set out determinedly to stand on her own feet. Now Nazim's own brother—if that was who he really was—seemed destined to force her to dance to his tune in the same way. History was repeating itself, she thought, her face cold and wintry.

She slanted a glance at Hassan. In the semi-gloom, he looked darkly menacing, only the snowy shirt and the whites of his eyes relieving the blackness clothing his body. He stared straight ahead, his classic profile carved from stone, as they took the Muscat road. There was a downward turn to his mouth and a sneer fractionally lifted the muscles of his face.

All that oozing charm and laughter with Josef had been false. He didn't like her, and there was no reason why he should like her son. Why, then, had he made contact with them both? Purely for the money? He could have done that without making a personal appearance.

Pride prevented her from asking. It would make it seem as if she was anxious or curious. So the head waiter himself had removed her coat—to an imperceptible intake of breath from Hassan, when he saw her no-holds-barred dress—shown them to a small intimate table, hidden behind greenery, and taken their order before Hassan spoke.

'You're desperate for work, aren't you?' he asked in a tone of velvet menace.

Assuming a cool and confident stare, Tiffany gave a slight shrug and looked as indifferent as possible. Her knee hit his thigh and she was aware of tightly muscled warmth beneath the soft wool of his trousers. The indifference slipped briefly. Their eyes met and she saw an unmistakable glitter of desire in his expression. She drew herself upright in her chair.

'Not that desperate,' she said calmly.

His mouth softened. Her pulses beat a little faster from an illogical sense of danger, mesmerised by the sexual threat pouring from his body, sweeping over her like a flash-flood.

'I could make you so successful that you wouldn't need to struggle for work any more,' he murmured, leaning forwards.

But there was an unpleasant ring to his voice and she wondered what the price might be. His eyes strayed to her bare shoulders and lingered with a chilling caress on the swell of her breasts. Tiffany felt hot and wanted to fidget, but kept her body utterly still, apart from taking quick sips from her glass of lemon tea.

'I don't think I'll have to struggle. Not as far as my work is concerned. It's good enough to warrant success,' she said coolly.

She handed him her designs. He abandoned the sautéd pigeon breast and flicked through the folder with narrowed eyes.

'Yes, it is,' he said unemotionally, without any evident enthusiasm. 'Here's the contract for the Omani project. I want you to handle it personally. Sign.'

Her lips parted in amazement and his dark eyes dropped to them, the lines of his face becoming filled with sensuality. A small quiver ran through Tiffany as her nerve-endings sprang into life. The heat in the restaurant was overpowering. It seemed suddenly cramped and claustrophobic. She felt her heart beating heavily. In confusion, she scanned his face, and found to her dismay that his expression only intensified her inflamed senses.

There was such uninhibited carnality flowing from him that it was like a brick wall coming straight for her. It was impossible to escape, impossible not to be affected. The gold of his skin glowed smoothly in the candlelight. The carved nose, chiselled mouth... every feature spelt out his sensuality and his hunger. The pulses hammered within her body, fighting the drugging seduction of his eyes.

She battled her way back to sanity, still mesmerised by him, but forcing her strong will to overcome the terrible and unwanted attraction she felt. She had glimpsed a vast, untapped well of passion within herself and it frightened her with its potential to destroy her calm, well-ordered life and self-control.

'Sign,' he drawled, with a mocking twist to his mouth.

'Sign?' she quavered, then frowned and tried to control her cracking vocal cords. 'Just like that?'

He smiled. Tiffany's heart fluttered alarmingly.

'Don't you want the work?' he asked in a husky voice.

She sliced fiercely into her Gravad Lax as if it were a tough steak and counted to ten.

'That depends on the price,' she observed coolly.

'I approve of your perception,' he murmured. 'You know I want something very badly. I could have it for the taking, I realise, but it would make things less distressful if you agreed not to make a fuss and give in gracefully.'

'I bet it would, you arrogant bastard!' she breathed, white with anger. He was certainly blunt! Hassan wanted her body, stretched out and willing on his bed. 'I have utter contempt for men who are in a position of power and make threats to control women.' She rose from the elegant chair, her body proud, the carriage of her head almost regal as she looked down her nose at him. 'In my country, we call that sexual harassment and it's punishable by the courts. Do your worst!' she said shakily, realising what she was having to do. The business she and Charlie had built up so painstakingly would be ruined by this man, merely because of his disgusting sexual appetite.

'You'll fight me for custody?' he grated, as she bent to pick up her handbag.

Tiffany froze. Then she felt her legs give way and she sat down again, dumbstruck with horror, her limpid grey eyes widened. He was serious. Deadly serious.

'For... what?' she whispered.

The strain showed in her face. She didn't delude herself. Hassan al Sharif, she knew, wouldn't look so sure of himself unless he had good reason.

'Custody,' he said in a chilling tone. 'Of Josef.'

'Jo? But... Oh, God! What... I feel sick,' she whispered, holding her head in her trembling hands.

He came over and poured water on a napkin, kneeling down and pushing away her hands and dabbing her forehead with it. Then, seeing she could hardly support herself in the chair, his strong arms went around her and his face was distressingly close to hers, harsh, relentless, his piercing eyes searing into her tormented soul.

For she remembered. It was something Nazim had said, soon after Josef's birth—and repeated often. In an effort to stop her from leaving him, he'd threatened to return to Riyam. She would lose her son, he'd yelled. Custody was almost always given to men in his country.

Could Nazim's brother do the same? Could he demand her son, as the nearest male relative? Her stomach knotted.

'You won't take Jo!' she whispered. 'You can't! We have English passports. Besides, you've given me no proof of who you are——'

'Here,' he said curtly, handing her his wallet.

With fumbling fingers, she flicked through the credit cards, the airline tickets, all for Hassan al Sharif, and stopped at a photograph of three men. Nazim. Hassan. And an older man in the middle, who appeared to be their father.

'Josef is *my* son,' she said levelly.

'I could get custody without any difficulty,' he claimed.

'Influential friends and the Sultan's blessing?' she asked, lacing her tone with heavy sarcasm.

'More than that. Already I have a great deal of information which indicates you are an unfit mother. But...' his hands gripped her wrists tightly as she opened her mouth to protest; she closed it when she saw from the triumph on his face that there was more horror to come '...it is the payment of a debt I have come for.'

The sick hysteria within her receded a little. Money. He was apparently rich beyond most people's wildest dreams. Yet he wanted what he'd obviously lent to Nazim, that time in Turkey. How much would that be?

She turned her head defiantly and met his liquid eyes. An inch more and their faces would be touching. Her pulses drummed in her ears.

'Get away from me,' she said with icy contempt. 'Take your hands off me. Their touch makes me feel nauseous. Sue me if you must. Your name will lose respect if you do, a man of your wealth forcing a widowed mother and her son into bankruptcy.'

His mouth twisted and Tiffany had the extraordinary feeling that he reluctantly admired her strength. Quietly, he returned to his seat and finished his food. Tiffany couldn't touch hers. There was another smile playing about his honey-moistened mouth, and his mocking glance flickered over her constantly, forcing her to remain in her seat. He had another ace up his sleeve, she knew, and waited in an agony of suspense. He'd string her out till she was screaming with nerves; he would take pleasure in taunting her.

The discreet waiter removed their plates and they waited in silence while his beef was flamed and she was served with her lamb.

'I have some news for you that will test that excellent English self-control of yours,' he said quietly. 'In fact,

I almost took you to my suite at my hotel, so we could be totally private, but I thought that unwise. For both of us.' His sultry eyes rested thoughtfully on her and she cut him with her glance. 'This was the best I could do,' he continued, indicating their privacy. 'Are you ready?'

'For anything,' she lied with a firm conviction. 'Tell me about this debt.'

'Very well. When Nazim contacted me, that time he was stranded in Turkey, I took advantage of the situation.'

'I bet you did,' she ground out.

He gave her an icy look. 'I arranged for him, his wife and child to be smuggled out of Turkey in exchange for the only thing he had of value.'

'You're too late if you want that consignment of Persian carpets. It was sold to pay off debts,' she said wearily. 'The money you lent him to set up again in England soon went.'

'It was a lot of money,' he frowned. 'It would take a great deal of extravagance to get through it.'

'I don't know how much it was——'

'Half a million pounds,' he drawled.

'Half——!' Tiffany gulped. She let out a sigh of despair. 'I can't possibly pay that back. There was a slump in the market for carpet importers. I have no cash to spare,' she said. 'Not now. But let me work on the project, without any strings attached, and I'll give you an agreed percentage to pay off what I owe you. I hate being beholden to anyone,' she added bitterly.

'Oh, you misunderstand. It's not carpets or money that I'm owed,' said Hassan huskily, pushing a document towards her.

Tiffany felt a change in the atmosphere. It had become tense and ominous. Her hand trembled as it took hold of the folded parchment.

'Well, if you're thinking to claim my body in part payment, it's not for loan, hire or sale,' she snapped.

Hassan gave her an indolent glance of sheer disdain. 'I'm not asking for it,' he said curtly.

Tiffany blushed. She'd thought...

'What was this item of value?' she asked coldly. 'Nazim had nothing. We were penniless.'

Hassan's face showed triumph. For several unbearable seconds, he kept her waiting for his answer, torturing her deliberately.

'What was it?' she cried in desperation. 'Tell me!'

'Your son,' he said softly.

'My son?'

'Well, to be legally precise, he isn't your son. He's mine. He belongs to me, you see. Nazim pledged him to me, as surety, to be surrendered if the debt was unpaid.'

Paralysed by what he'd said, all she could do was stare, her body as cold and stiff as if she were a corpse. And well she might be one, for all the life he had drained from her with his preposterous claim.

'He had no intention of repaying the debt,' said Hassan harshly, when she didn't answer, 'and to be honest, I banked on that, hoping to gain control of Josef.'

'Control?' she husked, aghast.

'Yes. To return him to his rightful culture, to people who could bring him up properly. But after a while I realised that, not only did Nazim not intend to repay the debt, he didn't have any intention of surrendering his son either. For a long time, I did nothing, giving him the opportunity to consider his position and honour his debt.'

'Nazim was right not to pay a debt of *dishonour*. My son isn't a pawn to be swapped around in payment, like a handful of coins!' Tiffany rasped.

Nazim had been even more of a worm than she'd thought. And so was his evil, callous brother.

He stilled her with a look.

'Someone had to rescue the child from his parents,' he scathed. 'I wish I'd done it sooner. I'd delayed because my father died and I was worked off my feet, taking over the business empire. He'd left it to me, not Nazim, the elder son, but felt all along that eventually the inheritance should also be Josef's. By then, Nazim had disappeared again.'

'How did you find us?' she asked resentfully.

'Pure chance. I saw the plans for your hotel and your name. I set out at once to discover if you were Nazim's wife, and, if so, what kind of woman you were.'

'And?' she breathed.

'My informants told me that my brother had died in a car crash,' he grated. 'They told me about the way you lived, in poverty, and that you'd provided no permanent home for Josef, wandering about Europe and Turkey like a vagrant.'

'I went where my work took me!' she seethed.

'Or your temporary...er...sponsors?' he queried. 'The men who put up the money for your fare——'

'They were reputable businessmen!' she cried hotly, flushing at his insinuation. 'Of course they paid——'

'For services rendered.' He nodded, with a mocking look in his eyes. 'You must have been exhausted, the hours you put into your job. I learnt you frequently were out at night.'

'Did you have me investigated?' she grated, incensed.

'I did,' said Hassan grimly. 'And I didn't like what I found out. I don't approve of a woman who spends money on expensive suits when her son goes about in rags.'

'But this is ridiculous! It's part of my job to have a good daytime wardrobe and to look smart——'

'This evening,' he continued relentlessly, 'my suspicions of your immorality were confirmed when I saw you with a man, silhouetted against your bedroom curtains in an intimate position.'

'Intimate——'

'He was on his knees,' hissed Hassan, his eyes boring into her. 'In my experience, that's pretty intimate.'

'Oh, for heaven's sake! I can explain——'

'Don't bother,' he growled.

She gave an exasperated sigh. 'He was getting an eyelash out of my eye.'

'You'd temporarily lost control of your hands?' he mocked.

'Yes.' She waved her fingers at him. 'I was doing my nails. They were wet. Mike is newly married and loves his wife.'

'I've seen her. She's not the sensual sort. He could easily be diverted by you,' said the sheikh in a low, matter-of-fact tone.

Tiffany faltered, disconcerted by the fact that he found her so attractive. It was flattering and worrying.

'Mike's in a rosy glow. He doesn't notice ... Why the hell am I defending myself to you?' she asked in irritation.

'I don't know. I don't believe what you say. Too much has contributed to form an unfavourable impression of your character.'

'So now you have this false opinion of me, what bearing does this have on what you intend to do?' she demanded.

The lines on his face grew harsher. 'It means I must take Josef from you. It's clear to me that he should be where he belongs. In his father's country, learning his true culture, being groomed to take over his inheritance when he comes of age.' He leant back in his chair. Tiffany could not move. Hassan sipped his iced water, his eyes never leaving her face, and continued. 'That document gives me the right to take Josef whenever I like. He is mine, given to me by his father. In law, you have no rights in the matter, and if you decide to fight me I will make life unbearable for you. I will *not* allow my nephew to grow up in a slum. I mean to give Josef the future he deserves. If you care anything for him, you won't stand in his way.'

'Really. And where do I fit in?' she grated.

'That depends. I could ensure that you never want for work over here——'

'Wait a minute!' she cried, galvanised into life. 'You take Josef, and I stay here? Is that your plan? You honestly think that I'd part with him?'

'For money and the sake of your career, yes. You seem single-mindedly selfish. And I certainly don't want you,' he said bluntly. 'I don't want your influence. He's reaching an age when he can do without you and needs the company of men.'

'This is a nightmare!'

'I don't think you realise the gravity of your situation,' said Hassan in velvet tones. 'As far as my country is concerned, I have unquestionable rights to Josef. It may take a little while for me to prove my claim, but I can certainly show that you're unfit with the evidence I have.'

'What evidence?' she asked in astonishment. 'Mike in my bedroom? I've explained that——'

'That, the fact that you sometimes come home in the early hours looking as if you've had a heavy night in some man's bed——'

'That's preposterous! Your investigator hasn't done his job properly. Very occasionally, I work at the studio half the night!' she said angrily. 'I have to put the hours in, to bring in enough for us to live on. Josef doesn't suffer; he's asleep. He's properly looked after. Mike and Mandy are very reliable and need the money as much as... Oh, damn you! I'm doing my utmost for him!'

He shrugged. 'Even if you can prove that, I can put pressure on in another way. I can call in the debt. You wouldn't be able to pay it and you'd go to prison. Josef would have no one to care for him. Naturally, with the other evidence I have of your unsuitability as a mother, I would be given custody then, as a relative who can offer him an infinitely better life than an impecunious jailbird,' he said softly. 'Heads I win, tails you lose.'

She stared in horror. 'You rat! You really mean it!'

His eyes blazed black and deadly. 'With every drop of my blood, every beat of my heart, I swear I will not allow Josef to remain with you. I'll have him, one way or another.'

For a moment, she was speechless, wilting beneath his blistering gaze. He hated her enough to tear her from her son. It was a prospect she couldn't bear to think of.

'I won't let you separate us! It's out of the question! You can't!' she whispered, her eyes filling with tears. Hassan frowned and concentrated on forking up some mange-tout as if they were discussing the ownership of a dog and not her son. 'I love him!' she moaned. 'He's all I have in the world——'

'You have your career,' he growled.

'Oh, God! Without Josef, everything is meaningless.' She saw a glimmer of hope. Hassan's hand had hesitated in mid-air. 'I beg you,' she said huskily. 'Leave us alone, to make our own way in life. You've managed all this time without Josef. You can run the business yourself. Pretend we don't exist. One day you'll have your own sons. We don't care about this inheritance. I love my son and will die rather than see him torn from me, or hurt in any way. For God's sake, he's a child! Believe me,' she said vehemently, 'I will defend him, no matter what the threat.'

The hand she had flung out in her plea, was enveloped in Hassan's warm grasp. He shifted closer to her and his knee slid alongside her thigh, but she didn't care. All she could think of was the danger to Josef.

'How passionate you are!' muttered Hassan, his eyes filled with desire. 'Your whole body is alive. Marrying you was the only sane thing Nazim ever did. You are the most beautiful woman I have ever known. And so feminine that your challenge to my masculinity is quite unbearable.' He turned her palm over and kissed it, branding her flesh with the heat of his lips. 'You are as graceful as a deer, as sensual as a houri. The perfect woman. A woman I am reluctant to abandon and see only in my dreams.'

'Please,' she moaned, incapable of withstanding his cruel, mocking seduction. 'Leave me alone.'

He gave a cynical laugh. 'See sense. Josef will be rich. He will have no need to go hungry or cold, or live in a rotting building. Josef will have better opportunities, better care with me, not a working mother who has to go out all day and half the night, and can't even clothe him properly. Can you deny him a bright future where he can use his talents to their best advantage? Can you deny him the chance to ride, ski, sail, even fly his own plane? What right have you to condemn him to a life of pinching and scraping? How do you think he will feel when he knows what opportunities are his for the asking?'

'You wouldn't tell him!' she cried hotly.

'Why the hell not?' growled Hassan. 'He has a right to know. It's his life you're thinking of ruining.'

'God, how I hate you!' she seethed, her beautiful face tense.

'That's understandable,' he said, with a mocking lift to his black eyebrow. Then he leant forwards. 'I have a legal right to Josef and a great deal of influence. I'll fight you in the international courts if you like, cite the presence of would-be lovers, expose your debts, cite your extravagance which Nazim complained of, and which plunged you all into a spiral of poverty. I'll show his letter to me, which complained that you trapped him into marriage through your pregnancy and that you insisted on following your career when your son was born. Is all that true?'

She gazed at him in dismay. An innocent and naïve eighteen-year-old, she had been Nazim's victim.

'Some, not all——'

'You bitch!' he snarled. 'The sooner Josef is out of your incapable hands, the better.'

'The facts have been twisted! I'm not what you think. You can't do this to us!' she hissed. 'He's settled in school——'

'He'll adapt. Children always do, if they're loved enough,' said Hassan ruthlessly.

She closed her eyes tightly, shutting out his harsh, savage face. Hassan had no mercy. He wanted his pound of flesh and nothing would stand in his way.

Silence fell between them as Tiffany sought to think rationally. At the moment, her mind was in such confusion that her judgement was impaired. She couldn't tell whether Hassan had a water-tight case against her or not. She didn't know enough of Arab law. The Shariah, Nazim had called it. And she knew that it was very much in favour of men, who played a strong part in the upbringing of their sons. But would the fact that Nazim had virtually signed away her son be upheld in English law?

Oh, God! How could he?

'I can't give up my son,' she said in a barely audible voice. 'If you insist on demanding your rights, then you'll have to fight me for him.'

'You'd ruin yourself to keep him? Turn down wealth?' he asked quietly.

It seemed he held his breath, waiting for her answer.

'I am not immoral and I have made every effort to care for him. Let the courts judge,' she whispered.

Hassan's expression remained impassive. He swirled the wine in his glass, thinking rapidly, a dark scowl on his face.

'I see,' he said slowly. 'I am surprised. I have failed to convince you that it would be in Josef's interest. It's a pity you feel this way.' He gave a gesture of defeat and Tiffany's hopes soared. Incredibly, she'd won! He'd given up! All that fervour had been put on to frighten her! Hassan sighed. 'I admire your strength. You have defeated me, it seems.'

'What...what are you going to do?' she asked warily.

'What can I do?' he countered. 'Would I really get involved in a court case which could last years? It would harm my nephew, and you could easily turn him against me. He'd hate me if I upset his mother. Would I be that stupid?'

'No,' she admitted, still uncertain. After all, he'd sworn that he'd stop at nothing... 'I suppose you've got too much sense to do that.'

'Well. That's that,' he said heavily. 'I must return to Riyam.' He sounded genuinely regretful. 'However... I must provide for him.'

'I'll accept no money from you,' she said, with a proud jut of her chin.

His eyes flickered. 'Foolish woman,' he growled. Then he gave a shrug. 'In that case, earn it.' He scrawled his signature on the Oman contract which he passed to her. 'I'll have a ticket waiting for you at the airport, by tomorrow afternoon, together with the necessary details. You can fly up the coast and see the site.'

Her grey eyes widened. 'What for?'

'I still need a designer. Why not you? Go there and clinch the deal with my lawyers. You can stay in the complex and look around; get the feel of it. I want you to stay for ten days and come up with some designs. Make a good job of the interior decoration and your fortune is made without any further help from me.'

'If I refuse?' she asked, her fine brows drawn together. 'If I want nothing to do with you?'

'You'd be that bloody-minded? Then I'll make sure you're broken if you wilfully refuse to take steps to give Josef a good life, even if that good life has to be without me. I'll make sure that every opening is denied to you, as it was with the Palm Sands deal.'

She shot him a look of loathing. 'You devious, manipulating rat!' she raged. 'You arranged for that to be cancelled, didn't you, so that you had a clear financial and professional hold over me? How low can you get?'

He gave a cynical smile. 'Pretty low. As low as I have to. Look at the sum your company will be paid.'

Tiffany stared. It was phenomenal.

'Well?' barked Hassan.

She let out a long breath. With that money, she could probably manage comfortably. But…he was forcing the pace again. Making her rush about whenever he snapped his fingers. It galled her to jump to his bidding, yet she'd be stupid to refuse. It seemed the only way to keep her head above water and survive this ghastly nightmare.

Otherwise, she thought miserably, he'd carry on with his underhand vendetta and Josef would have to leave his beloved school. She'd never be able to afford the fees.

'How do I know this is above board?' she asked sullenly, her mouth unconsciously pouting.

'Check with the Omani Embassy in the morning,' he said curtly. 'They'll vouch for the scheme, and me.'

'Why are you helping me?' she asked doubtfully. There must be a snag, but for the life of her she couldn't find it.

'I'm not. I'm helping Josef,' he snapped. 'He is of my blood.'

She tossed her head in a defiant gesture. 'I can't just leap up, pack my bags and go away for ten days. There's Jo to consider. I need a little more notice——'

'No. Leave tomorrow night, or not at all,' he snapped. 'That is my price. Explain to him what it means to you.'

She teetered on the edge of accepting. It was so tempting, the opportunity for so much. Everything she'd worked for lay within her grasp. She could check with the embassy that the development existed.

'You want every last bit of my humble pie, don't you?' she glared, her eyes slate-hard.

'Is it much to ask? I need to salvage a little of my pride,' he shrugged, 'since I will be returning home without my nephew.'

She realised that he hadn't expected to fail in his mission. He'd imagined she'd turn her son over to him, lured by the prospect of money. But who would look after Josef if she went?

Almost immediately, an idea occurred to her. His burning ambition could be realised. He could board at the school! Now, she could afford that. He'd be thrilled! Though she must warn the school not to allow him contact with anyone apart from herself. She had time to go there tomorrow and tell the headmaster that Josef must be supervised. Jo would be in his element; he would be with friends, and well cared for, and she could concentrate on the job in hand.

In a swift movement, she rose, leaving her meal untouched on the table. Her stomach was in no fit state for food. It kept lurching about virtually every time Hassan let out another devastating bombshell.

'I accept,' she said with a frosty stare. 'Don't bother to see me home in that ostentatious piece of scrap metal outside. I'll take a taxi. If I'm leaving for ten days, I have some explaining to do to Josef and a great deal to organise.' A thought struck her, and she paused, suddenly apprehensive. 'You are returning tonight, aren't you? You're not waiting till I leave the country and then go sneaking off to kidnap Josef?'

His chest swelled in offence as he stood up and fixed her with an outraged expression.

'I told you, I am leaving. On my soul, I would not dream of snatching Josef and causing him distress. I care for his welfare, unlike you.'

She was reassured. But as she stalked haughtily through the restaurant, her spine tingling from Hassan's watchful gaze, the doubts began to crowd into her mind and she wondered whether she was doing the right thing after all.

CHAPTER THREE

TIFFANY landed at Sohar at noon, two days after the fateful dinner with Hassan, weary from lack of sleep the night before, the frantic rush to tie up everything at home and a rapid top-up of her wardrobe. Charlie had been dumbfounded, but his delight that they might stay solvent had carried her through the hasty handing over to him the last few pieces of work remaining for the hotel.

She should have been feeling elated that the next year was financially secure, but she didn't. There was a strange flatness inside her.

The intense heat—unusual by the coast—was doing its best to flatten her, too. She longed for a shower to cool herself down. Not long. Cool herb tea and nutty pastries beckoned.

She followed an airport official across the tarmac, pulling down the brim of her straw hat against the glare of the dancing heat. The sun burned into her arms, exposed beneath a short-sleeved jacket-style cotton top, but a warm breeze moved her full skirt and gave a welcome relief from the intense blast for a while.

Boarding the small jet which was to take her to the development site, she was surprised to find it took off almost immediately and that she was the only passenger. The drone of the engine lulled her to sleep and she woke with a start when the steward quietly asked her to fasten her seatbelt for the landing.

The beautiful sleek Mercedes Benz which met her was blissfully air-conditioned. She felt partly refreshed from her sleep and examined the harsh landscape with interest through the smoked windows, hanging on to the leather strap as the driver swung along the desert road and chatted on his handset at the same time.

It seemed a long journey, through arid scenery with not a building in sight apart from a ruined caravanserai. To her surprise, they stopped at this, and the driver got out and leant against the car as if waiting for someone.

Tiffany eyed the man warily, then clambered out, meaning to ask what he was doing. As she did so, she saw him stiffen and shade his eyes.

She followed his gaze. Far into the distance, she saw the small, indistinct figure of a solitary rider. He was surrounded by a haze of heat and a cloud of dust. His shimmering white robes merged with the snow-white horse to give an impression of one pagan creature. She smiled faintly at the magnificent sight.

As the man neared, she could see that the horse was at a full gallop and the rider lay low in the saddle, guiding the animal swiftly and surely between the massive rock boulders strewn across the wild landscape. Man and beast were in perfect harmony, a fusing of natural animal grace.

Her secretly romantic nature thrilled to see the stallion's long mane streaming back like white ribbons, and his powerful muscles bunching and stretching. It was such an arresting sight that it didn't occur to her to wonder why the driver had stopped to await the advancing rider, nor what purpose the rider served.

Quite near now, and probably showing off, the veiled man had eased the breakneck pace and was lounging in the saddle. He was shrouded in a long white robe, edged with gold braid, and a traditional bedouin head-dress. His black desert boots were slipped into gleaming silver stirrups, hanging over bright red leather saddle-bags, and his hands lightly held the colourfully embroidered reins.

To her delight, the huge stallion was reined in near her. He fretted and pawed at the ground, evidently sulking that the glorious gallop was at an end.

Tiffany smiled at the rider, her graceful hand pushing back a strand of sun-gold hair which had escaped in the warm, dry breeze. His eyes were narrow slits, as she imagined all desert men's must be, and were only just exposed above the tightly wrapped cloth which had been flung across his face against the choking dust. His hand rested momentarily on the butt of his rifle which had been thrust into a deep saddle holster, then he gathered the reins purposefully in his hands.

Tiffany made to turn, thinking that the display was over and she would resume her journey to the coast. But the rider had jabbed his heels hard into the stallion's flanks and was making straight for her.

'*No!*' she screamed, realising in a split second what this must be. Hassan's revenge!

She flung a frantic glance at the curious but motionless chauffeur, as the massive horse bore down on her in a thunder of flying hoofs. She saw his eyes roll, his bared teeth, and then she was being whisked up into the air.

Rough, cruel hands crushed Tiffany's body as, rigid with terror, she was swung across to the rider's lap. Her hat fell off; the horse skittered, then she felt the hard steel of male thighs beneath hers.

And most unnerving of all was the vicious grip which held her a prisoner. So frightened was she that she could only scream soundlessly. Her whole body trembled, bending like a supple willow as she realised she was totally at the man's mercy.

Her eyes slowly lifted and a violent shock ran through her.

Hassan.

Tiffany's stomach lurched. She'd recognise those glittering jet-black eyes anywhere. Especially as they were laced with a savage hatred and a look of malice which pierced her body like a repeatedly stabbing knife.

'Hassan!' she croaked.

He laughed. 'Hassan,' he agreed mockingly.

She felt his thigh muscles tighten and swell as he brought the horse under control. One of his arms slid from her body and she was forced to cling to him, afraid of falling, hating the necessity of clutching at his chest like an adoring, desperate woman.

'What are you doing?' she yelled up at him.

He reached out and lifted the loose reins, collecting the horse. It seemed to her that suddenly man and beast became one hard, efficient powerhouse of energy, working in perfect unity, honed muscles rippling, wild natures barely held in check.

In a brief flash of realisation, Tiffany became truly aware of Hassan's immense kinship with the desert and all things natural, pagan, wild. And it terrified her.

'What are you doing?' she repeated with an authority she didn't feel.

'Abducting you,' he growled.

She cringed within.

'You can't! Josef——'

'He's safe at school,' he laughed. 'Whereas you have a different lesson to learn.'

Hassan's body throbbed with vitality and he seemed elated, causing her nerve-endings to spring to life. He was exuberant because he had a foul plan in his mind and its success seemed assured. She wanted to weep. The safety of her tiny flat, Charlie and Josef seemed a long,

long way from this malevolent man and this hostile environment.

He leant forwards, holding her tightly, his right arm unnervingly stretched across her breasts, his fingers splayed insultingly over the rising swell.

Automatically she strained away, but the arm tightened over her ribs and she was crushed into a solid wall of unresisting muscle and bone. The long, tanned fingers pressed deeper into her side, and as the horse gathered pace his spreading thumb regularly met her rhythmically bouncing left breast.

'Hassan! Please!' she cried, finding her voice. It was torn from her lips by the wind and the heat, emerging like a choked sob.

'Save your breath!' he grated. 'You'll need it. Every last gasp.'

She dared not struggle. He was perfectly capable of letting her drop to the ground. She glanced down. It looked a bone-breaking distance away.

To Tiffany's frightened eyes, the stony desert stretched far ahead, glinting in the relentless sun, barren, featureless. She was in his territory now. He intended... She gulped, her imagination examining a number of possibilities.

'This won't get you anywhere!' she managed, feeling melodramatic as she shouted in the direction of the venomous eyes above her.

She felt his grunt reverberate through his chest, and then he had spurred his stallion on, bending her unwilling body with his dominant one as he leaned low against the wind, emphasising his authority and her submission. The weight of his head lay on her shoulder, the pressure of his chin bruised her flesh.

She felt an increasing apprehension about Hassan's highly physical presence. His body dominated hers in more ways than one. Alarm made her quiver as she re-alised his fast, heavy breathing and the rapid thudding of his heart were not entirely caused by the effort of riding.

'Now let me go!' she ordered. 'Stop this ridiculous attempt to frighten me!'

'Ah. Success. Is that what I'm doing?' he murmured into her ear, with a rush of hot breath.

Tiffany flushed, recalling the avid sensuality of his hot eyes when they had virtually stripped her the night she'd been wearing her kimono. He was capable of violence, with all those fierce passions held so tightly in check. He'd be like his brother.

Nazim had always seemed quiet and controlled on the exterior, only the terrifying way he had first made love to her betraying the savagery within him. And later had come frequent displays of his violent temper.

Her white teeth dug hard into her lower lip as the memory made her shudder with revulsion.

Hassan let out a low grunt. She was really afraid. He must know every curve of her figure by now. How shaming. If he was as lusty as his brother, he'd be quick to arouse. After all, she'd only permitted Nazim to kiss and caress her and he'd turned into a tenacious, un-stoppable lecher.

Hassan wriggled slightly in the saddle, making her aware of every potent inch of his body beneath the thin cotton robe. And, to her dismay, he tucked his face against hers so that they were cheek to cheek, the fine material of his head-dress doing nothing at all to conceal the strong bones of his face and the fiercely clenched jaw.

She wrenched her head away, but it was too uncom-fortable to stay in that position for long and soon it nat-

urally returned to lie against that despised face, though
every muscle in her body stayed tense.

'Relax,' he muttered. 'There's nothing you can do at
all. Nothing.'

'Just you wait!' she retorted hotly.

Relax! While she was being abducted, fondled in the
most insulting way! Tiffany drew in an angry breath,
inflating her ribcage, and regretted it immediately as she
felt a movement in his cheek muscles and realised he was
grimacing at the result. For her breasts had risen, and,
beneath the flimsy material of her dress, had settled
themselves so that their peaks were being rhythmically
massaged against his arm by the motion of riding.

To her horror, she felt heat course through her body,
engulfing her in its flames. And no amount of arching
her back could disguise the fact that her breasts had
swollen, and their tips met Hassan's welcoming arm with
an increasingly hard pressure, till they felt as hard as
bone and as sensitive as her wildly leaping nerves. Tiffany
moaned.

'Patience,' mocked Hassan. 'Control your needs.
Enjoy the ride.'

'You rat! Stop touching my body!' she yelled back at
him, her eyes fevered.

'It's that, or fall,' he snarled. 'Keep still and don't
tempt me.'

'You're disgusting! Loathsome! You enjoy humiliating me!'

She tried to change position, and became alarmed at
the heat in his loins which burned shockingly into her
buttocks. Her whole body went rigid. The horse stumbled
on a pebble and the iron band of Hassan's arm swelled
as the muscles expanded and held her firmly, with even
greater intimacy than before. Now she was completely

plastered against him and no secrets of touch remained between them.

'For your own safety, keep still,' he muttered. 'For my own sanity, don't *move*.'

The flames in Tiffany's body simmered wilfully. Unable to bear the constant survey of Hassan's embered eyes, she turned her head and buried it in his chest, hoping he would sense her feminine vulnerability, and pity rather than desire her. Cradled against the soft cotton robe which soothed her cheek, she breathed in the surprisingly pleasant scent of his hot male body, which was mingled with the faint perfume of rose-water.

'Let me go!' she moaned into the folds over his chest.

'Not yet.' His voice murmured through her hair. 'Not till we're alone.'

Tiffany gulped. 'Alone?' she husked, barely able to say the word. 'Where? Why?'

'Let your imagination run riot,' he said sardonically.

She did and it made her tremble uncontrollably.

His breath exhaled harshly, hot and tingling as it riffled through her hair and sensitised her temples. The big hand adjusted its hold, moving away from her breast, but still splayed in arrogant possession across her fragile ribs, claiming her for his own.

Tiffany tried to make her mind forget the disturbing sensations and think what action she might take when he stopped. There was no point in trying to run away; he was bound to be taking her somewhere isolated. Her only hope lay in appealing to any remnants of civilised behaviour he might have. She frowned. That wasn't much. Her lip refused to stop quivering.

Clutched in his ruthless arms, she felt incredibly vulnerable. She wouldn't have much chance against him if he tried to rape her.

When she refused his advances point-blank, her delicate bones could easily be crushed by a blow from that massive, cruel hand. Misery filled her eyes. Old memories of pain, from Nazim's petulant slaps, rose to sicken her. She bruised easily. Violence made her physically ill.

'Sheikh Hassan. I appeal to your sense of honour——' she began shakily.

'Shut up,' he snarled savagely, yanking hard on the reins.

The stallion jerked his head alarmingly, flicking back foam. Hassan gave an exasperated grunt and spoke to him in gentle, soothing tones which hummed through Tiffany's ribcage in a resonant rumble. He leaned to the right and the horse obeyed the sway of his body, trotting into the dry torrent bed of a river. It was surprisingly deep, and edged with tamarisk trees which rose directly from the pebble bed, as if they scorned anything as soft as soil.

A chill settled on her. This was a harsh land, where only the harsh survived. It was like Hassan himself. Beneath his sophisticated, smooth exterior lay an uncompromising lack of softness. In Hassan's heart lurked a nature in harmony with the unrelenting desert, a man equal to the task of surviving here in the most inhospitable surroundings, pitting his wits against nature itself. What chance did she have, with someone so accomplished in winning against all odds?

A shudder rippled through her, and Hassan's hand began to move, gently stroking. Its invasiveness made her shrink. Instead of soothing her, it was, she felt, causing the panic rising within her chest. And, she thought bitterly, struggling in his arms futilely, his touch brought her dormant sensuality to life.

Her whole love-starved body was tensing against his insistent caress. The hollowing physical need of a body incomplete because of its lack of a satisfying union mocked her shocked mind. She raised a flushed face to his, breathing with shallow gasps.

'You bastard! Don't touch me like that!' she grated.

'You don't want to be calmed down?' he murmured.

'I *am* calm!' she yelled.

He grinned, his eyes crinkling up above the veil.

'Lucky you,' he said softly, bending his head down.

Tiffany strained back, swaying alarmingly as Hassan adjusted his hold on her, laughing as he did. She was incensed. Part of that anger was for herself. When he'd bent his head, she had wished the barrier of his head-dress didn't exist and their lips could have met for one brief, crazy second.

Her eyes were drawn to the faint outline of his mouth through the fine cotton. It became serious. She badly wanted to drag her gaze from his lips, but seemed to be incapable of doing so. She clenched her jaw to prevent the overwhelming urge to wrap her arms around his neck. Her mouth felt parched for tender kisses.

A spasm of hungry pain lashed through her, condemning her wanton thoughts. This was what he had planned—an excuse to hold her with the utmost intimacy, her gradual awareness of his intense sensuality and her eventual surrender. Then he would be able to use his sexual hold over her to gain what he really wanted: Josef.

Tiffany's warmth turned to ice. Guilt and shame washed over her. Hassan's attraction was so insistent that she had allowed her instincts to respond, rather than keeping her head clear. Whatever he did, whatever he said, he had one aim only. She could not allow herself to be fooled for one moment.

Unconsciously, Tiffany had drawn her body into a ramrod posture. Her head had lifted from its position against Hassan's chest where his heartbeat pounded so unnervingly fast and furious. He was aroused, that was embarrassingly evident, but now Tiffany felt strong. Coldly she suffered his unwanted embrace, her spine stiff, her face staring into the middle distance with a tight, closed expression.

'Thank you,' he said drily.

Startled, she flashed him a frost-bitten look, but he was serious. It puzzled her and she was left wondering what he meant.

They followed the river bed's twists and turns. Then she felt the tension of his muscles beneath her and he drew her upright body firmly into his.

'Stop that!' she yelled. 'I told you, I loathe your filthy hands——'

'Hold on tightly.' His hot breath hit her ear harshly, making her spine shiver with the sensation.

The horse was forced up the steep side of the wadi and she flung her arms around Hassan's waist, clinging on for dear life as the stallion slipped and slid on the polished rock-face. Above them, coming into view as they began to make their way up the slope, was a cluster of palms in a boulder-strewn desert, and behind them, rearing in a jagged wall, were stark mountains which stretched across the whole horizon.

The ringing sound of iron hoof on stone echoed in the vast empty desert, emphasising the unnerving loneliness she felt. They moved beneath feathery tamarisk, brushing beneath the twisted branches, and the unbearable heat on Tiffany's head disappeared.

As they came to the shady palms at a walking pace, she wriggled her hand from around Hassan's waist and felt her scalp. It was burning.

'I'll get sunstroke because of you,' she accused.

'Your hat fell off.'

As if that explained his lack of sense!

'You callous brute!' she snapped. 'Are you trying to kill me?'

'You survived, didn't you?' he growled.

His arm withdrew from her ribs and he stood in the stirrups, settling her in the saddle firmly. Then he swung down in a lithe movement, slowly unfolding the material wrapped around his face.

Tiffany eyed him warily, knowing her legs wouldn't hold her if she tried to stand. At least she was safe on the horse. There wasn't much he could do to her there, apart from touch her. Dismounting promised a greater danger.

'Get down,' he ordered, raising a hand to help.

'What for?' she snapped.

He scowled. 'Because my horse needs to recover. He's the only thing that stands between us and death. If he falls, we're done for. The next waterhole is forty miles away. Well?'

Oh, God! What was he planning? 'I can manage,' she muttered, pride getting the better of sense. 'Move aside. I don't want your sweaty hands anywhere near me.'

His black eyes flickered dangerously, but he moved back with a mocking bow. Tiffany grabbed the pommel of the saddle and dismounted. But her strong will wasn't enough to prevent her knees from buckling and she staggered.

Hassan didn't move. She flung out her hands to the ground to save herself from falling, grazing them on the sharp stones. Ignoring her smarting palms, she rose on trembling legs and faced him squarely.

'You cold-hearted monster!' she seethed.

He was smiling cynically. 'Don't glare. Much as I wanted to help, I respected your wishes. You said you didn't want my sweaty hands to touch you,' he remarked, moving towards her.

She shied away, but he had only come to see to his horse. She watched as he removed the saddle-bag and then the saddle, and loosened the girth, then spent some time seeing to the stallion's needs before he was satisfied and let the horse trot off to the water-filled channel which led into the pool a few yards away.

Tiffany licked her dry lips as she heard the stallion's muzzle swishing in the water.

'Cool yourself down,' said Hassan curtly. 'We're staying for ten minutes only.'

'Ten!' Tiffany's eyes blazed. 'I'm hot and thirsty and determined not to budge from here until you tell me just what you expect to achieve by this childish act.'

'Oh, it's not childish,' he murmured, unravelling his head-dress. 'And I don't think you see me as a child, either, do you, Tiffany?'

'No, I don't,' she agreed, her lashes lowered, knowing that there would be a satisfied smirk on his face. 'I see you as a foul and brutish animal.'

His sharp exhalation made her look up—and that was a fatal mistake. Hassan al Sharif made an arresting sight. Framed against a backdrop of gently waving palms in a searingly blue sky, he stood with his black desert boots planted firmly apart, his powerful shoulders squared in anger.

But it was his face which hypnotised her. In this setting, he was even more compellingly handsome than before. His hair lay blue-black and damp against his scalp, curling slightly where the head-dress had constricted it. Rage and pride shaped the lines of his face, bestowing on them a harsh beauty which caught her breath.

His eyes brooded on her, pure black like the desert night, touched by a glint of silver fire which glittered dangerously. Tiffany couldn't look away, captured by the softening light which was changing the darkness of his eyes into a glowing warm velvet shot with stars.

Her lips parted, forced to do so by her rapid breathing. She took a step backwards, moistening her dry lips so that she could speak.

In two strides, he had covered the distance between them, and then he checked himself with an effort.

He flung his head back, breathing in the clean desert air noisily. And then his hooded eyes flickered down to where she stood like a bewildered gazelle, hypnotised by a predator.

'Refresh yourself,' he growled. 'Then you can change.'

'Into what?' she asked shakily, fighting for sanity. The desert was making her act crazily. 'A dancing girl? Your whore? Or would you prefer the added spice of resistance from your prisoner?'

'Don't be ridiculous!' he roared. 'Refuse to act sensibly if you must, but we'll be riding on in a few minutes whatever you do. And in two hours you'll wish you'd taken a drink and that you'd put on the clothes in my saddle-bag. Do as you're told.'

He swung on his heel and strode purposefully towards the pool. Resenting the truth of what he said, Tiffany drank from the channel which ran with fresh spring water, and splashed her head and neck with it, cooling herself down. A saddle-bag was flung at her feet and she studiously ignored it, wondering how she could change while he watched.

'Dress.'

'I won't be part of a floor-show for a half-crazed Arab,' she snapped, quivering a little at his appearance.

Water glistened on his skin, giving it a silver sheen in the sunlight, and the black hair dripped small pearl-shaped, sparkling droplets. His wet robe clung to his body like a second skin, forcing her to acknowledge the unnerving breadth of his chest and the well-developed muscles there. She dared not lower her eyes further. He was drenched. The thin cotton had done little to conceal his body beneath when it was dry. Now... She swallowed nervously.

He regarded her sourly. 'Before I show you what a *completely* crazed Arab is really like,' he said with soft menace, 'put the clothes on.'

Sullenly she bent down and undid the buckle. Inside there was a large amount of fine black cotton material, neatly folded. Sulkily, she drew it out. Beneath lay a bright peacock-green Arab tunic and trousers. Her wary eyes turned to his, as her fingers sank into the soft, delicate material. It was disturbingly flimsy.

'You expect me to wear this?' she asked slowly in disbelief. 'Are you really asking me to dress up like an Arab girl?'

'I picked those clothes,' he drawled, 'because, strange though it may seem to you, after a few thousand years of living in the desert my people know the most suitable garments to wear. They will protect you.'

'From you? Then I'll put them on immediately!' she said scathingly. 'But it strikes me as odd that you should bother to protect me when I've been in the sun without a hat for so long. It's hardly surprising I'm suspicious. Maybe you have an ulterior motive for making me strip.'

'You weren't in any danger,' he retorted. 'It was a short journey and your hair is thick, especially piled on top of your head like that. But now we cross the dunes and the heat will be intense. It is a long ride, Tiffany, some hours. You'll need every ounce of energy in your body to endure that.'

Her eyes widened. 'Hours?' she cried in dismay. 'Why, Hassan, why? Where are you taking me?'

'I'll tell you when I'm ready. Now hurry. We began our journey at an unfortunate time of day.'

'All right,' she said grudgingly. 'I'll protect my head with the black chador, but I won't put on the clothes. I'm darned if I'll play the part of your Arabian concubine!'

The black eyes narrowed ominously. Before Tiffany could turn and run, he had come up behind her and yanked open her jacket, pulling it down over her shoulders so that her naked back was exposed to the hot air and his equally hot eyes. Effortlessly he turned her around to face him and his big hands gripped the material, effectively trapping her arms.

Then her chin was gripped between his finger and thumb and tilted up, so that she was forced to look into his fierce eyes.

'Stubborn woman! Recognise what is best for you!'

'Never seeing you again would do for a start,' she seethed.

'Tiffany, I can strip off your clothes and those small lacy briefs you are wearing, in this undignified way, if you continue to insist on defying me, or you can be sensible and dress yourself. I will have no compunction in ripping this garment from your body. Whatever happens, you'll ride into the desert with me and you'll be wearing the clothes I have chosen.'

His voice was low and menacing. She had winced at his mention of her briefs. It enraged her that he knew so much about her body. He had held her with too much intimacy on that damn horse of his.

'You are without doubt the most bestial, most degenerate devil I have ever had the misfortune to meet,' she said coldly. 'Now turn away and show me that you have a vestige of human decency in you.'

'Tiffany——' he began.

'Turn away!' she cried hysterically, believing that the low-spoken word was the start of the seduction she feared. Her outburst worked. He frowned and went to prepare his horse.

But she didn't trust him. As if she were undressing on the beach, she draped the chador over her head like a tent and slipped her dress off. She discovered that the green outfit was balm to her hot flesh. When she had positioned the black garment over it, covering her head completely, she thought ruefully that they would look like man and wife to any stranger who saw them riding together.

'I'm ready,' she called flatly. Hassan led the stallion to her. 'And I want to know where we're going.'

'Eventually to my home,' he said, his eyes travelling up and down her figure in approval.

She cringed. 'No! Why——?'

He shook his head impatiently. 'We haven't time to discuss it. Here.'

His hand reached out and caught the end of her veil. If she pulled away it would be ripped, and she'd be left only with the close-fitting harem outfit to wear. Helplessly she stood while he drew the fold across her face, his eyes mocking her as he did so. His long, elegant fingers delicately fixed the end into a small hook which she hadn't noticed.

Mutely she waited, wishing his breath wouldn't fan her face in that sensitising way, wishing he didn't have such thick, fringing lashes and such an unfairly primitive appeal. Wishing... She gulped.

Slowly, the lashes lifted and his eyes slid to meet hers. The fingers hesitated, hovering above the veil. His lips curved sensually and her own mouth parted in response to the hunger within her.

'Mount,' he said in a whisper.

Tiffany blinked, trembling, wondering what it would be like to be kissed by a man like Hassan, and rooted to the spot in confusion at her thoughts.

'God! You shouldn't have hesitated! Where the hell has my resolve gone? Tiffany,' he muttered huskily, 'I am unable to resist you. Every movement of your body has aroused me so that I can hardly contain myself. Damn you! Damn you to hell! You and that gorgeous body of yours have driven me to this!'

'Hassan...' Her throat shut off.

A lazy desire flooded his face, and she was so afraid and the flooding weakness was so overwhelming that her limbs refused to move, refused to let her run or even make any further protest.

She had been hypnotised, she thought numbly, watching the sweet parting of his arching mouth. With a delicate, lingering movement, Hassan unhooked the veil and deliberately let it float across her face, causing her skin to tingle with its gossamer touch.

'No,' she croaked, her eyes huge, and as clouded as a troubled lake.

But his strong head bent relentlessly and, as it did so, her lips lifted instinctively to his in a desperately pagan need, as if the desert had drawn from her all the layers of civilisation and left her only with primal desire. Dry, aching, she needed her raging thirst to be quenched. And Hassan was the man to satisfy the barrenness in her body.

The kiss was as deep as a well, as violent as a deluge. His mouth was cool and firm, moving with determination over hers, flowing smoothly, and she found herself responding eagerly, nothing but an impulsive passion driving her willing lips to seek relief from thirst.

Within her, it was as if a dam had burst. Inhibition had left her, defeated by the incredible hold Hassan had over her. And he seemed content to match her unbounded demand. Her fingers faltered on his shoulders, then drifted longingly over them, revelling in their strength and the curve of his back as it bent to her.

He was beautiful. Perfect. The man of her dreams.

Tiffany felt her body glow and become fluid, obedient to his masterful kiss. Then she jerked violently and stiffened. For he had begun to coax her lips apart and she remembered the disgust she had felt when Nazim had invaded her mouth so ruthlessly. Her whole being shuddered with revulsion.

And then the pressure of Hassan's body had gone. She lifted her heavy lids which had closed without her knowing. Looking at him with confused, dewy eyes, she thought he seemed pale and strained.

For several seconds they stared at one another, and then he passed a hand through his damp hair, not taking his eyes off her for one second.

'How much more humiliation do I have to take?' she whispered with scorn. 'You've made your point. I am at your mercy. My body is yours to assault, to rape. My life depends on you entirely at this moment.' Her glacial eyes searched his and saw him flinch. 'But whatever you do to me, Sheikh Hassan,' she said, gaining courage, 'you'll never touch me inside. My mind and my soul are mine and can't be hurt by you. If you plan to harm me, you might remember that.'

His mouth twisted and his expression became unreadable. He linked his hands and indicated she should get into the saddle. She vaulted up and he took the reins,

walking along beside her in long, heavy-heeled strides
as if he was taking out his temper in physical activity.

She refused to think. Didn't want to. Whenever a
vision of Hassan, brutalising her, came to her mind she
shut it out with a fierce effort of will. Josef was waiting
at home for her. She would come through all this,
whatever it might be. She would return home to him and
close her mind to this terrible experience. Whatever it
might be.

The saddle creaked beneath her and soon she became
mesmerised by the steady, monotonous rhythm and the
never-ending dunes which stretched into the far horizon,
to the foot of the soaring mountains.

Hassan strode on, relentless with himself in the heat.
It seemed nothing touched him, she mused, her re-
sentful eyes lingering on his tense back and lowered head.
He seemed to have the capacity to withstand any discomfort, scornful of normal human frailties like
exhaustion.

She began to slump and found her back aching dread-
fully. Her legs chafed, too, and she let out a gasp of
discomfort as the stallion side-stepped to avoid a snake
which Hassan had ignored.

'Tired?' he asked curtly, over his shoulder.

'What the hell do you think?' she snapped.

Without a word, he slipped the reins over the horse's
arching neck and motioned for her to take one foot from
the stirrup. He swung up and squeezed into the saddle
behind her.

'Lean back,' he ordered grimly.

She wouldn't. Instead, she strained forwards.

'God! You're stubborn!' he muttered.

He crushed her against him and she was wrapped in his arms, her spine supported by his chest. It was blissfully comfortable after the strain of the last hour.

The sun blazed hotter and hotter, hitting the stones among the dunes like an anvil. The rays glanced blindingly back into their faces and she was glad of the veil that protected her. She was incapable of speech, her throat as dry as the sands.

Hassan adjusted her chador as they rode, so that the folds lay thickly over her head, then tucked one huge hand around her middle. Around them, the dunes sparkled with colour—orange, gold, rose, silver, as the grains reflected the sun. Despite her distress, Tiffany began to understand why some people revered the desert landscape.

It was true that it could be harsh and merciless. But it was also very beautiful. There was something pure and clean about the scene, as though the mountains and dunes had been cut out and stuck on a hard blue background. It was all so uncluttered, and the sense of space was majestic.

But the monotony of the pace made her drowsy. Several times she felt her head roll and Hassan's arm tighten around her. Eventually she longed for a change of pace to keep her awake.

'Can't we go any faster?' she asked irritably, her voice hoarse and cracked.

'We could.'

He did nothing to back up his answer. Her nerves rose to screaming pitch. She wanted this terrible, interminable journey to end so that she could know the worst.

With an impatient mutter, driven almost insane by the situation, she clapped her heels into the stallion's flanks. It took off immediately, launching himself into a full gallop. Tiffany clutched at the saddle with a scream. It was drowned by Hassan's roar. His body tensed as he fought to hold the animal.

In a moment they were stationary. Tiffany sat sobbing, overcome with an intense misery at the situation.

'Let me go home,' she moaned. 'I want my son. You can't separate us. You can't really mean to threaten me——'

She broke off as the lump in her throat prevented her from saying any more.

'This matter is far too important for me to be swayed by your tears,' rasped Hassan. 'The mountains are near. It'll be cooler soon. Let me decide how to get there and don't make my horse half kill itself by galloping in this heat again.'

'You care more for your horse than for people,' she said sullenly.

'Some people don't deserve my concern,' he growled.

'What have I done?' she asked, astonished.

'You ruined my brother,' he bit out. 'And I won't have my nephew brought up to be as callous as you.'

'I don't know what you mean,' she said wearily. 'You've jumped to conclusions——'

'Shut up. We'll have it out soon. I want to know everything about you. You'll tell me every detail of your life. Then I can decide whether you accompany Josef to Riyam or not.'

'But you admitted to defeat——'

'No. I said that it seemed as if I was defeated. Not that I *was*.'

Her mind whirled back to what he'd said. She went over it all. 'You have defeated me, it seems. What can I do?' The back of her neck prickled. Hassan was a dangerous man, devious and clever.

'Josef will live with me,' she said icily.

'Rest. You're tired. We'll talk about it later.'

Tiffany groaned. The heat was sapping her strength and her will. She could hardly stay awake. The mountains did seem closer. But at the moment, they were absorbing the sun's rays and throwing them back at her. The air was breathless, with an ovenlike heat she could smell. The sun now hung like a huge white ball in the sky, and the haze in front of them made the dunes appear to shimmer like heaps of diamonds.

She slept. Waking, she found herself cradled in Hassan's arms. He gazed down on her with worryingly softened eyes as she jerked upright and shivered in the chilly air. The sun had become a baleful crimson, staining the desert the colour of blood.

It was magnificent, glorious. Massive clouds hung stacked like red and purple blankets. It was the most incredible sunset she had ever seen. Her head turned to view the great coloured canopy over their heads and she marvelled at how insignificant they were amid its vastness.

Her normal world, that of the city, seemed narrow and confining. The horizon had always been bound by buildings, enclosed, and looking in on itself. She'd never known how immense an empty space could be, nor how beautiful.

Her eyes gentled and a languid feeling of peace swept over her, the warm strength of Hassan's encircling arms infinitely appealing. The setting was mesmerising her, playing on her yearning sensibilities for love and romance in the vacuum of her life.

'One of the three really breathtaking sights in the world,' murmured Hassan's deep voice, 'and a tantalising glimpse of infinity.' His breath fanned her face. 'It puts us in perspective, doesn't it?'

She nodded slowly, caught in the magic of the moment, watching with awe the great clouds roll across the heavens and seeing the crimson sands turn wine-dark.

'And what are these other breathtaking sights?' she asked quietly.

He was very still suddenly, as if he were somewhere else entirely. Then he spoke, so softly that she could hardly hear his words.

'A woman in love, and the face of a child,' he said huskily.

Tiffany felt her heart contract at the simple perfection of his answer. It had been beautiful, almost poetic, and utterly sincere. She trembled, aware that she had trespassed into his private, sensitive self.

Then she felt suddenly much more confident. If Hassan nursed thoughts like that, he couldn't be the monster he pretended. There was hope. A spark of humanity existed. She could appeal to his sense of justice and honour, and, if that failed, to his sentimental heart which placed children so highly. Unconsciously she relaxed into his arms.

They trudged up a steep crescent-shaped dune, and when they topped it she saw the dark shapes of palm trees, outlined in a black silhouette against the yellowing sky. The oasis was set in what appeared to be a huge salt-pan. She closed her eyes against the intensity of the light and then after a while the glare receded on her eyelids. Expecting to see that a cloud had passed over the setting sun, she found that they had left the desert and were passing beneath lush palms.

Eagerly she looked around for signs of habitation, a fort maybe, or small lime-washed houses, but there was nothing.

'Is this our destination?' she asked uncertainly, peering ahead into the thick plantation.

He gave a small laugh. 'No. This, Tiffany, is where you and I are going to get to know one another.'

Her face tightened with nerves. 'What do you mean?'

His eyes bored into hers.

'I mean that this is where we will spend the night. Just the two of us.'

CHAPTER FOUR

SLOWLY Tiffany turned her head to scan the scene. They were totally alone.

She had been expecting to arrive at his house by nightfall. Without knowing she did so, she'd hoped for a civilised, sophisticated house with servants, a place where she could appeal to Hassan's westernised side. It had never occurred to her that she would be trapped with him in the desert. He was a different man here.

So it was in this pagan setting that Hassan planned on acting out the climax to his little scheme. Whatever... She felt her throat constrict and she thought ruefully that her body seemed to know things before her mind did.

Of course. He wanted it all: Josef, her, and the complete success of his plans. His pride would accept nothing less than that; he'd want her to admit he had absolute power over her. And how better could he display that power than by sexual domination?

God, she was stupid, to let herself fall in his hands like a ripe plum!

Her eyes spotted the rifle in its deep holster which was buckled to the saddle-bag. The butt was close. If she could . . .

'Tiffany,' came Hassan's sardonic voice, 'it's not loaded. Forget it.'

'Never,' she vowed. 'Never.'

But her words belied her weak body. Misery, fear, hunger and exhaustion caught up on her in a black, sweeping wave. Her brain was careering around inside

her head like an out-of-control carousel. Through a dark
fog she felt herself being lifted from the saddle, and the
next thing she knew was that she lay on the ground and
Hassan's fingers were fumbling with the neck fastening
of her tunic.

'No! Don't!' she cried hoarsely.

'Dammit, Tiffany, I——'

'How could you?'

She fought him like a wildcat, using her nails where
she could, yelling in her terror, the material tearing and
exposing part of her breast. With a moan, she drew the
torn cloth to cover herself.

'Leave me alone!' she screamed, flailing with her
hands.

Hassan's rough hands let her go and he got up, to
stand glaring down at her as she lay in a tumbled heap
on the ground.

'You bully!' she whispered, staring at him with pained
eyes, her body turned to ice. 'I despise you!' she ground
out vehemently with all the passion of her being. 'More
than anyone I've ever known!'

He fingered his shoulder where she'd dug in her nails.

'Hell! You seem to have recovered with a vengeance!'
he growled.

'I hope it hurts. Try that again,' she seethed, 'and I'll
tear your face apart.'

'Get up,' he barked, his eyes blazing. 'Stop jumping
to the wrong conclusions and stop being melodramatic.
Bring the food from the saddle-bag. I'll light a fire. Obey
me,' he said in a warning tone, as it looked as if she
intended to defy him, 'or you go hungry. And I'm very
tempted to abandon you right now. What chance of your
survival without me?'

Holding her body erect, every disdainful inch showing
her contempt, she stalked over to the well. Without a

word spoken to her, he unhooked a silver scoop from his belt, which she dipped in the leather bucket, pouring the sparkling water over her head and body. She felt vehemently that she must wash away the imprint of his marauding hands.

Numbly she collected the saddle-bag. She had to eat. There were a few hunks of bread, some cheese, fruit and dates. Nothing else.

'Are you trying to starve me, too?' she shouted at him as he strode away.

His big body turned and he eyed her silently. Then his chest inflated with a deep breath.

'Anyone who eats heavily on a desert journey is a fool,' he said, and spun on his heel.

She glared at his retreating back and ate half the food, eyeing the rest with longing, but she didn't dare to touch it. She feared him. Damn him!

Hassan was some time. Tiffany waited, wondering where they would sleep. That was, she thought, with a gnawing agony inside her, if she was allowed to sleep at all. He had said that he wanted to get to know her. Her tongue slicked over her upper lip. It was unlikely that he meant a civilised chat.

However much she had to admit that he had briefly aroused her base desires—and hated herself for that humiliating fact—she dreaded what might come next. Hassan gave off an aura of such virility that she knew instinctively he would have an insatiable appetite. She'd gone through the pain of a man's animal lust before. She couldn't stand it again.

Her head aching, Tiffany drew the chador from her head and unpinned her hair, releasing the tension in her scalp where the grips clustered among the heavy strands.

Sex. It began pleasurably; it ended with disappointment. To her, it had been a perpetual sensation of emptiness, a nameless loss and failure, which pervaded her whole being and made her feel cheated. She never wanted to have that sense of despairing frustration again.

There was a sound ahead of her. She blinked in surprise, seeing that night had fallen as swiftly as if a light had been switched off. The utter darkness was unknown to her and she felt unnervingly vulnerable. It seemed to wrap her in a stifling cloak of dark velvet.

Hassan came into sight, pausing when he saw her. His flowing robes were white against the blackness, and above his head were the tiny flickering stars, looking for all the world like minute gemstones.

Tiffany steeled herself to her forthcoming ordeal.

'I've lit a fire,' he said abruptly, then turned his back on her and strode away.

Well! she thought, in astonishment. That wasn't the behaviour of a man who had evil designs on her! Emboldened, she hurried after his retreating figure.

The fire glowed comfortingly and she huddled close to it, suddenly cold, and thinking she ought to go and get the black robe—not that it would have been much good, because it was so thin. She looked back in the direction of the well where she'd stupidly left it.

It was very dark. She didn't want to search for something that would be so little use.

As she crouched by the fire, the front of her body soon became warm, but her back remained chilled. Hassan moved about busily, setting a brass-beaked coffee pot on the fire. She wondered how he had the energy, after urging his stallion and a reluctant hostage over miles of unfriendly desert. A scowl crossed her face. She resented his indifference to the elements.

'I'm cold,' she said, wrapping her arms around herself. The peacock-green outfit shimmered in the firelight as she massaged her arms.

'It'll get colder,' he commented indifferently.

'So what are you going to do about it?' She frowned, then her eyes rounded as she realised that she'd given him an opportunity to tell her just what he would do to warm her up!

He slanted his eyes at her shivering body, the lower part of his jaw dark with beard now.

'You want me to change creation?' he asked mockingly. 'To make the desert warm at night for you?'

Relief flooded her face. She really would have to be careful in her choice of words. It seemed, however, that his mind wasn't on her body after all, or he would have taken up that challenge.

'I want something to wrap around me. Are you purposely depriving me of civilised comfort? Is this intentionally vindictive behaviour on your part?' she asked with scorn. 'I suppose you've read *The Taming of The Shrew*, and fancied putting some of Shakespeare's ideas into practice!'

He poured a stream of thick black coffee from the pot into two tiny brass cups and handed one to her.

'Are you really so used to living with all the benefits of modern life that you can't appreciate simplicity?' he countered, ignoring her jibe.

'You saw my flat,' she said sullenly.

He scowled. 'Yes. Squalid, wasn't it?'

'It wasn't that bad! You try being a penniless widow with an eight-year-old son!' she snapped.

'Don't feel sorry for yourself. You got yourself in trouble.'

She flushed scarlet. It wasn't her fault that she had become pregnant by Nazim. How dared he? She tried to think up something rude to say, but her brain was tired.

He sat cross-legged on the ground. He was a little too close for her liking, but she pretended that it didn't bother her and stayed where she was. She had no intention of letting him know she felt intimidated.

'I hate to think of Josef living under such appalling conditions because of your stupidity,' he said tightly. 'My God! You really made him suffer!'

She drank the hot sweet liquid before answering, irritated that she'd given him some more ammunition for his attacks on her.

'My son never went hungry or cold,' she said with quiet dignity. 'His diet might not have been as good as it is now, but he ate healthily, I saw to that. You can't deny that he's a smashing kiddie. And if his clothes were second-hand, they still kept him warm. I tried to give him the best education we could manage, so that he has the chances I didn't.'

She looked up at him defiantly. Hassan's face looked drawn. His bleak eyes met hers.

The trunks of the palms and acacia trees around them creaked and complained as they contracted in the cold. The heaped sand beneath the palms whispered, disturbed by a light breeze. The thin new moon had risen and shone its light on the crystalline crust beyond. Tiffany shivered at the eerie scene.

'Let's get down to business,' said Hassan grimly.

'*Business!* Is that what you call it? You unemotional swine!' she scathed.

'I want Josef,' he said bluntly.

A chill raised the hairs on her spine. 'So that's it! You're holding me hostage! The Batinah project was a ruse to bring me here, then,' she said bitterly. 'How could you raise my hopes about the future for Josef and me? You got me here under false pretences!'

'Not entirely. You can work on the scheme. I told you; it's yours for the taking. I'll fly you there as soon as you like.'

'Providing...?' she grated, with a querying eyebrow.

'Exactly,' he said with a grunt of satisfaction. 'I want your co-operation. When we arrive at my home, I want you to ring Josef up at the school and tell him you want him to fly out to us both. He'll come like a shot. Won't he?'

'Well,' she said sarcastically. 'It's all nicely worked out, isn't it?'

'I think so,' he said, with a maddening smile.

It didn't reach his eyes, though. They remained utterly hostile, as hard and glittering as black diamonds.

'And me?' she asked, her voice wavering. 'Where do I fit into your neat little scheme?'

'I told you before. Nowhere. I want you to gradually fade out of his life.'

She quailed. She'd been wrong about his intentions, then. He wanted only Josef, and she was to return to Seeb or even England, without her son, if his plans came to fruition. He was very single-minded, very determined, and his hatred of her was absolute.

'Aren't you afraid that when we reach wherever you're taking me I'll somehow give you the slip?'

'No. My fortress is impregnable. If I choose to keep you there, you won't escape. And since it's my bolt-hole, it is remote, in the middle of the desert, with no way in and no way out apart from the air, or this long, beautiful caravan route.'

'Beautiful?' she scathed. 'It's tortuous.'

'You hate my country?' he frowned.

'*Your...?*' Her senses sharpened. 'Wait a minute! I had the impression that we were going to a home of yours in Oman! Are you telling me we're in . . . in Riyam?' she asked, her nerves climbing to screaming-point.

He smiled mockingly. 'Correct. The plane brought you straight here. This is Riyam. My country. And it seems that even on a short acquaintance you hate it.'

'Damn right, I do!' she cried, hiding her dismay by her attack. 'And its people! Particularly its arrogant, ruthless men! You enjoy wielding power over women, don't you? Using physical strength and bullying tactics to intimidate and frighten! Well, Sheikh Hassan, you might harm me, but you won't get my son. And I swear to God you won't ever crush my spirit!'

But he was close to doing so. The dark night hummed around her. She was trapped. He'd won. Riyami laws applied here. He'd take her to his fortress and no one would help her; no one would dare to. If she didn't agree to his demands, she'd probably never see Josef again. The prospect was appalling.

Hassan's eyes were warm on her, shining, she thought, with the light of grudging admiration, and that irritated her.

'Tiffany,' he said quietly, 'understand why I'm doing this——'

'I don't!' she cried hotly, tossing her hair with impatience and frustration. 'Why would you take a son from his mother? Have you no decency at all? No finer feelings?'

She'd angered him. His big chest had risen and his face was thunderous.

'I'm thinking only of Josef,' he snarled. 'He must come first in all of this. My information is that you, his mother, lured my brother into casual sex and then forced him to marry you by using blackmail.'

'No——'

'You ask me to believe you, rather than my own brother?' he said with a proud tilt to his head. He leaned forwards, contempt written all over his face, and Tiffany despaired of ever proving herself innocent. 'He wrote and told me all about you, remember. That you tried to kill your own child, and when that didn't work you sulked all through your pregnancy.'

'I was ill——'

'You are not fit to be a mother of any child, let alone my nephew! Apart from your hatred of motherhood and facing up to your responsibilities, there is the additional charge of wild extravagance and promiscuity. Is it any wonder I want Josef and will go to any lengths to get him? How do you think I feel, to know my brother's son, flesh of my father, blood of my blood, is learning about women and life through your roaming, amoral eyes?'

'But you're basing your actions on hearsay!' she cried vehemently.

'Not only that,' he continued, ignoring her interruption as if she hadn't even spoken. 'Your sluttish behaviour in your own home, with Josef in the next room, convinced me that I was right. I can recognise a woman who breathes sensuality from every pore. Normally I make no judgement on women like you—but you are corrupting an innocent child.'

'I deny everything you say about me,' she grated. 'All of it. Josef is happy with me——'

'He knows nothing else,' snapped Hassan. 'Listen to sense. Josef has every right to know of his father's culture, to be introduced to his only remaining kin. He has a right to live in comfort instead of poverty. You won't go away empty-handed. I'll see to that. It's a good bargain, Tiffany.'

'But here! It's so barren...'

Distaste on her face, she waved an expressive arm at the desert surrounding the oasis.

'Riyam is a country of contrasts,' said Hassan. 'Like its people. The desert has its own beauty to those who look. We have lush green valleys and oases too, full of plants and birds.'

'And you'd train him to be like you,' she said bitterly, making no secret of the fact that she thought that would be the worst thing he could do.

Hassan's brows lowered. 'I would make sure he was interested in the business and teach him how to handle it. And how to deal with people.'

'Oh, that's easy,' said Tiffany sarcastically. 'The Sharifs find what they love, take it, or threaten it. Then they have the power to do what they like.'

His teeth clenched hard. 'Only when the situation is desperate,' he grated.

'Desperate?' She glared. '*You're* desperate? How the hell do you think I feel?'

'You'll get what you always wanted,' he said stubbornly. 'Your freedom. I know you wanted that from the start, that Josef's birth came between you and your plans. You can pursue your career—and I have made a promise to you that my influence will put work your way. In a few years, you could be very wealthy from your talent. You'd like that, wouldn't you? You've never made a secret of the fact that you're career-minded.'

'I find it fulfilling, yes,' she said in exasperation. 'But what would that be, without my son? Knowing he was being taught your unethical methods of manipulating people, changing from the child I know to a ruthless, empty-hearted man like you?'

Hassan's temper began to fray and Tiffany felt she were sitting in the middle of a brewing storm. Between them, hostility crackled like an electric charge as they both fought for what they wanted.

'For God's sake, Tiffany!' he rapped. 'Stop pretending to be a devoted mother. Are you holding out for a share of my wealth? Admit that you were horrified to discover you were pregnant. Admit that you didn't want your child, that you tried to have it aborted——'

'No, no! That's not true!' she cried in despair.

'You almost lost your baby——'

'Yes, I fell...' She choked. 'Nazim pushed me, overcome with temper, after my mother told him I was carrying his child.'

A glacial light flickered in Hassan's eyes.

'You bitch! Now I am certain that you lie,' he said with soft menace. 'Because no Arab would ever do anything to harm his child. A child is sacred, Tiffany. You're blackening my brother's name, knowing that he can't defend himself. Well, I defend him as a Sharif, and despise you the more for making Nazim bear your own failings. I know that all through your pregnancy you were miserable, and insisted on trying to continue at art school. And even after Josef's birth, you were determined to continue with your career and couldn't care less about looking after your son!'

'You would stick up for him!' she raged. 'You would believe him, before me! It's all lies! Of course I was upset to find I was pregnant! I was unmarried and didn't want——'

'You didn't want a child to inconvenience you,' he said tightly.

'I give up. It's no use talking to you,' she said wearily. 'You'll never believe me.'

'No. I won't. What you think doesn't matter, anyway. Give in. You're beaten. Let's make Josef's arrival here a harmonious one, not with the two of us at daggers drawn, so that he's torn in half by our antagonism. If you really loved him, you'd agree. Besides, Riyami law will uphold my claim to him. Co-operate, or Josef will suffer,' he said grimly. 'I'll have him, whatever you do. Of that, I'm certain. Do it the easy way, or the hard way. It's your choice.'

'The judgement of Solomon, all over again,' she whispered. 'My son will be cut in two if I stand up for my rights. And I lose him if I don't.'

Her head lifted and she stared into the darkness with moist eyes. What chance did she have of fighting Hassan, now that she was here? He was without mercy. To make his point, he would cleave Josef apart.

'You're intending to keep me prisoner until you have what you want.'

He didn't answer her statement. She made a helpless gesture.

'I agree,' she mouthed, unable to speak the words aloud. 'On one condition.'

Tears sprang from her eyes, cascading down her face as misery rose to conquer her self-control. Somehow she'd get herself and Josef out of this mess. But for the present...

'You're in no position to make conditions,' he growled.

'Listen to me!' she begged. 'I'll make it easy for us all by accepting the inevitable. I'll do anything you ask. Only let me stay with my son. If you have an ounce of pity within you, grant me that. You've beaten me. I give in to your foul demands. But be generous in your victory. Oh, God! Don't deny me the right to stay with my own son, my own flesh and blood. He'd be unhappy without me. I couldn't bear to think of him pining.'

She raised her tear-stained face, knowing that her sanity depended on his answer. Her heart would be broken if she never saw Josef again. Anything, even living as a virtual prisoner of this merciless man, would be preferable.

Separation would be a torture more violent than mere physical blows. She couldn't keep her shaking body still. Her emotions had been ripped to shreds. She tipped her head back in hopelessness at the situation she was in. Her hair fell like a golden river down her back.

'Please,' she croaked. 'Oh, please, please, Hassan! I beg you from the depths of my heart!'

The stars twinkled cruelly at her from the vast black canopy, making her feel very lonely. There was a deep silence, so intense that it seemed her ears ached with it. The slow flames on the fire licked at the acacia, which filled the air with aromatic scent.

'I couldn't trust you,' he said in a slow, thoughtful voice. 'You'd have far too good an opportunity to make Josef hate me. It wouldn't be difficult for you to persuade him that life in England would be sweeter. You and I would be strangers with opposing aims, quietly destroying Josef between us. You see, there would be nothing that bound you to my purpose, nothing to ensure you made a genuine attempt to help Josef adjust to life with me.'

Tiffany wanted to scream. He hadn't refused outright. He was weakening in his resolve to send her away, but she didn't know how to make him relent. He wouldn't want to be seen to lose face. Curse his pride. What could she do?

'Oh, Hassan!' she moaned, feeling her chance to see Josef grow up slip away. 'If you ask me to crawl on hands and knees, I will if I have to. I have a hell of a lot of pride, but not where my son is concerned. You profess to care about him; can't you see that he'll be unhappy without me? I've brought him up; you're asking him to start a new life in a new country without the one person he loves.'

'I don't want him unhappy. I don't want you to crawl,' he growled.

She grasped his arms and threw every ounce of her heart into what she said.

'What do you want, then? Ask me. I'll do it. I'll do anything! Anything you want! Name it, it's yours!'

His wickedly white teeth drove deep into his lower lip. 'Anything?' he repeated hoarsely.

Shudders ran through her at the naked desire in his voice and the sexual threat which sent her nerves singing. Now that he had Josef, his mind and body were turning to her. Nazim's demands would be nothing compared with this man's smouldering sensuality.

'Even...' His hand reached up to touch her cheek. Tiffany closed her eyes tightly. 'You see, there is only one way. You would even give yourself?' he murmured.

The very air became charged with his raw need, surrounding her in its relentless seduction. It made her shrink into herself with an involuntary movement.

She didn't dare to stop him. Not yet. She must not make him angry. Once she had his agreement, she could make it clear that she wanted nothing to do with him and that he'd have little pleasure in forcing her against her will. It was a slim hope, but one she had to believe in or she'd crack up.

His fingers pushed gently through the silk of her hair. A touch like a butterfly's wing trailed across the bones of her face, over her neck and along her shoulders.

Hassan's face had lost its cruelty, its granite-hard determination. Now he was all man, flesh, blood, beating pulses. The desire driving from his body terrified her.

'You're so beautiful,' he said huskily.

She flinched. The warm, soft pad of his thumb outlined her quivering lips with all the skill and expertise of a master at seduction. And, more than she could have believed possible at this terrible moment in her life, his dark, sultry eyes and potent masculinity were awakening her stupidly responsive body as his relentless fingers sought her arousal.

Tiffany groaned. She'd never felt this kind of need before. He was using her hollow, unfulfilled womanhood with skill, knowing his expertise, relying on the lure of the promise of satisfaction which poured from his skilled fingers and his knowing eyes.

The cruel knives of desire were driving into her and she had to dig her hands into his shoulders to prevent herself from crying out. She had to get away from her own destructive longing. Another shudder ripped through her.

'You ask for that?' she whispered.

'It's what I want, at this moment,' he growled.

His mouth had a sultry arch which all but mesmerised her. She felt that her turbulent emotions were no longer under her control.

'God!' she breathed, incapable of understanding why her body melted at the mere thought of his naked body. It was indecent. Unladylike. Unstoppable.

'You said anything. That's what I want. You,' he said in a remorseless tone. 'Hell!' he groaned. 'Whatever I think about you, my eyes, my hands, my lips seem incapable of keeping off your irresistible body. I am obsessed by you, Tiffany. I have been consumed with desire for you since that day I first set eyes on you and I loathe you for that alone. I must either get rid of you, or take you. There is no middle way as far as I am concerned. The fierce contrasts of the desert. It's all or nothing.

And I want all. Till you have nothing more to give and I have nothing more to take.'

His mouth touched her throat, forcing her head back, and she felt the burning of his lips on her flesh. Tiffany fought the unwelcome surges of warmth in response to the savagery beneath his gentle assault. Her head strained back in an effort to increase the distance between them.

'I couldn't surrender and keep my self-respect. You'd have to rape me,' she warned in terror, her breath coming fast and heavy.

'No. I wouldn't. You'd join with me in enjoying every touch, every movement. Every new path my fingers, my lips, my teeth, my tongue, may find.'

'No,' she denied, every inch of her tingling with anticipation.

His palm splayed out on her back and ran down the soft material, making her hollow her spine away from his touch. It was impossible for her to stop trembling. Deep within her lay a pool of molten heat, waiting to rise in her veins, waiting to erupt in an explosive surrender.

And she wouldn't allow it to. She tensed her whole body.

'Submit to me,' he murmured against her ear.

'No! I won't,' she moaned.

'Then you are of no use to me,' he said softly, staring into her eyes.

She slicked her tongue over her lips and, mocking her, he did the same to his. An agony of sweet pain coursed through her body. She wanted him, God help her, she was hooked by the first man who'd managed to arouse her. Sex seemed to have more impulsive, irrational power than sense.

'For the last time, let me stay with you and Josef!' she whispered. 'Don't degrade me, your own sister-in-law, by demanding my body as a payment.'

He held a lock of her hair and was rubbing it sensually between his finger and thumb, lost in its silkiness. A sinful ripple ran through her veins, making her breath quicken and her lips part softly.

'I want your submission, Tiffany. I want you to offer yourself to me.'

'No,' she whispered.

How she hated him for what he was doing to her! she thought bitterly. He was making her come to terms with the fact that she wasn't cool and controlled at all, beneath the surface. Hassan's charismatic sensual nature had destroyed all her barriers like a heat-seeking missile.

He was in complete control of his sexuality and was able to use it to his advantage. Tiffany screwed up every muscle in her body, hoping to dissipate the shameful desire she felt for him.

'There is one alternative,' he said slowly.

Tiffany grasped at the straw of hope.

'Name it,' she snapped, giving him a hard look. 'Anything would be preferable to being abused by you.'

His lashes hid his expression and he dropped the strand of hair as if he'd been scalded.

'There's only one way you can stay with Josef if he is in my house. I do see the wisdom of letting you remain with him. Maybe after a while you won't wish to stay; we can come to some arrangement about that. You could have respect, and my protection. You would have a considerable influence over Josef's upbringing and a life of comfort.'

She was almost willing to let him ravish her, if it meant all that. Her protective instincts towards Josef were fierce enough to do almost anything to keep some kind of say in the formation of his character, so that he didn't turn out as dissolute as his father, or as ruthless as his uncle.

'What would I have to do?' she asked in a chilly whisper.

Hassan smiled hungrily. 'Become my wife.' She gasped and made to speak, but the grip on her arm stopped her. 'Not a bad exchange, a veneer of respectability, for spending days and nights of pleasure in my bed, is it?' he said with a voracious look.

Days and nights? she thought in horror.

'Wife number one? Two? Three?' she snapped scornfully.

He shook his head. 'I am a Christian, of course. The Sharifs have been Christians for a hundred years. One wife at a time,' he said with a low laugh.

'Why... why bother to offer me this farce of marriage?' she asked. 'You could force me.'

'I could indeed. But I want you like hell. I want your abandoned responses. I want absolute surrender and to know that you find my lovemaking impossible to resist. I want you to beg me to take you, to need me. I want to see you weak and defenceless from my kisses. Only then might my obsession fade. Until that time comes, when I tire of you, our union will be infinitely more enjoyable if you are willing,' he growled huskily.

'I'd be passive, not willing!' she declared hotly, tossing her shimmering head.

He laughed again, his teeth dazzling white, and she resented how handsome he looked when he did so.

'Your body would never allow you to stay passive,' he smiled.

She stared at him in silence. He was right. It wouldn't. But her head would hate every second.

'You want it all, don't you?' she said in an acid tone.

'Oh, yes. I want it all. I've never gone for anything less. Well?'

'What choice do I have?' she said bitterly. 'You know I'm forced to agree. It's the most barbaric, cold-blooded proposal. If I don't agree, you'd keep me here anyway as a revenge, wouldn't you? And if I never went back to Oman, the authorities there would have to send Josef back to England or put him into a children's home. We'd lose each other if I refused your monstrous suggestion. Oh, yes, I agree. But with every inch of my body I resent doing so, and hate and loathe you for putting us in this situation! How clever you've been. You'll have no legal battles. No expensive, long-drawn-out court appearances, no sullen nephew who's missing his mother. And, on top of all that, you have me to paw any time you choose.' Incensed that he had cleverly managed to get everything he wanted, she fixed brilliant steel eyes on him, her voice husky with emotion. 'I agree, you bastard. Just remember that I won't pretend to like you and I won't pretend to enjoy what you do to me.'

'Oh, I think I'll overcome your reservations,' he said softly, his mouth lightly running down her cheekbone. 'Easily,' he growled. 'I'll make you forget Nazim's lovemaking!'

She gave a deep shudder, remembering. 'No,' she said in tones of ice. 'I won't ever forget. No woman could. That will remain in my mind and my body till my dying day!'

Hassan went very still, and when she looked at him she saw he was white-lipped. His hands dropped away, pain shadowing his eyes. She had, it seemed, successfully fended him off. He disliked thinking of her and his brother. It doused his arousal effectively. She must remember that. It could be her only defence.

'I have your word?' he asked grimly.

'Yes.'

She felt better now. He could be diverted from assaulting her. She had very little to hang on to, but now she wouldn't entirely lose Josef. It was better than nothing.

'Then get some sleep. Make a hollow in the sand to fit your body. It will be warm underneath the cold surface,' he said in a distant tone. 'Try to rest. We ride early tomorrow.'

She stared at him, trembling.

'You're not . . . you're not going to . . .'

His eyes gleamed in the darkness.

'You want sex?' he asked, in a hard voice.

'You bastard! No!'

'Your mind is overcoming your body at last,' he mocked.

'I loathe you, Hassan al Sharif, brother-in-law or not,' she grated. 'And don't you forget it!'

She scraped furiously at the sand to make herself a warm hollow, relieved that he was settling down a short distance away.

'Don't you have a blanket for me, or anything?' she asked, when she'd finished.

'No.'

He rolled over, turning his back on her. Soon there was that dense silence again, the kind of silence that broke the nerve.

Tiffany curled up by the fire, turning her body this way and that, trying to get comfortable, trying to keep every part warm, and failing. Fatigue claimed her limbs. She lay in a lethargic, frozen daze, miserable, unable to stop her teeth chattering.

Her spirits were low. A small sob broke free of her lips. Hassan rolled over with a grunt.

'Hell. What's the matter?' he asked curtly.

'I—I'm cold and miserable. What the devil d-do you think is the m-matter?' she stammered through her sobs. 'You've stripped me of all d-dignity and forced me into a horrible marriage.'

'Come here,' he snapped.

'You're *evil*!' she cried, with all the feeling she could muster.

When Hassan came over and stood above her, she stared numbly at the pair of black boots, too tired to do anything. If he took her now, he'd get little pleasure, she thought dully.

He bent down and picked her up, still curled into a ball, and she was so worn out that she couldn't even struggle. His strength of mind and body was impressive.

A long, blood-curdling howl echoed through the clarity of the night, and then another. Tiffany gasped and her arms flew around Hassan's neck. She buried her head in his shoulder, shaking violently.

'Don't be afraid, Tiffany. It's only wolves,' he said gruffly. 'In the mountains. Now to sleep. I'm tired, even if you aren't.'

Against the glorious warmth of the hollow of his shoulder, she tightened her mouth angrily. But she let him lower her to the ground and settle himself with an impersonal efficiency, drawing her to him so that she rested her head against his heart. And her eyes were closing against her wishes, her mind becoming drowsy, and she slept almost immediately.

Some time in the small hours, she half woke, to find Hassan's hands wandering over her body. He was muttering something in Arabic which she didn't understand. But she did understand what he meant to do. Imprisoned in his arms, she wriggled her hands free to defend herself.

Resisting, his fingers slid to explore the curves of her waist and she pushed against him forcefully.

A hand drifted to her thighs and she felt the old sensation of panic she had felt when Nazim had reached that point.

'Oh, God! Don't touch me! I'll feel sick,' she moaned.

Hassan's eyes snapped open, startled.

'What is it?' he asked muzzily, his face unnervingly close to hers. 'What's the matter?'

Although he released her immediately, she remained defensive and bristling with outrage.

'You were mauling me,' she said furiously.

His face became cold. 'I didn't know. I was dreaming,' he muttered.

'Of your dream woman, I suppose,' she scathed. 'A female who is always ready and willing, who enjoys your touch.'

The light was dim, but Tiffany could have sworn that his skin became faintly flushed.

'Do you still feel sick?' he rasped.

'Not any longer. Not now you've stopped fondling me,' she answered with a baleful look.

His brows drew together in a savage scowl. 'It's not long till dawn. There's no point in trying to sleep. We'll ride on,' he said abruptly.

'Oh, no!' she cried in exhaustion, tipping her head right back.

She should never have done that. Before she knew what was happening, Hassan had given a groan and had pressed her back to the ground. His mouth drove into hers ruthlessly, taking her breath away in a bruising kiss which her body welcomed if her mind railed against it.

Fiercer and fiercer his mouth ground down, and, under his passionate onslaught, her own lips began to respond in desperate need, devouring him, her hands lacing into

GET 4 BOOKS

Return this card, and we'll send you 4 brand-new Harlequin Presents® novels, absolutely *FREE!* We'll even pay the postage both ways!

We're making you this offer to introduce you to the benefits of the Harlequin Reader Service®: free home delivery of brand-new romance novels, months before they're available in stores, **AND** at a saving of 30¢ apiece compared to the cover price!

Accepting these 4 free books places you under no obligation to continue. You may cancel at any time, even just after receiving your free shipment. If you do not cancel, every month, we'll send 6 more Harlequin Presents® novels and bill you just $2.49* apiece—that's all!

Yes! Please send me my 4 free Harlequin Presents® novels, as explained above.

Name

Address   Apt.

City   State   Zip

106 CIH ADGQ (U-H-P-11/91)

DETACH ALONG DOTTED LINE AND MAIL TODAY! – DETACH ALONG DOTTED LINE AND MAIL TODAY! – DETACH ALONG DOTTED LINE AND MAIL TODAY! – DETACH ALONG DOTTED LINE AND MAIL TODAY!

Get 4 Books FREE

SEE BACK OF CARD FOR DETAILS

his glossy dark hair and driving his head hard downwards so that all the terrible passion within her could be released. His mouth slid over her jaw and then returned, tenderly this time, drifting tantalisingly so that it just touched her skin, while his hand lifted to fondle the nape of her neck. A thrill of sensation shot down her spine and she gave a small moan.

Hassan spread out her golden hair on the sand, lifting it from her nape with delicate, incredibly electrifying movements of his fingers on her scalp. She luxuriated in the freedom and sensuality that this gesture gave her, small, throaty moans escaping from her in wanton, uninhibited ecstasy.

Hassan's languid, long forefinger lifted to the corner of her mouth, sliding delicately, tortuously over the soft down of her cheek and sweeping back to press her murmuring lips. Her chest tightened at his caress. It was gentle, tender... She whimpered. Her whole body seemed to be welcoming him. And no wonder. He knew instinctively how she wanted to be touched, and that his hands and lips were slowly but surely increasing her arousal to an exquisite level.

'I tried,' he whispered. 'God help me, I tried!' His mouth slid, kiss by kiss, to the lobe of her ear. 'I know this is unfair. That you hate me. But... I want you. Heaven is my witness, I want you!'

'Please——' she tried to protest, feeling a spear slice through her at his impassioned words. He sounded shaky and driven by dangerous desire.

'Tiffany!' he groaned, devouring her ear. 'Tiffany... Let me ease my madness for you. Let me please you,' he coaxed. 'I've wanted this for too long.'

She jerked in response to the incredible sensation of his lips and tongue. Suddenly, her mouth was covered by his in a fierce, never-ending kiss that took her breath away. She sank willingly into its warmth, crying aloud for him, her arms frantically holding him, enjoying his strong body as she pressed herself boldly against him.

Aching inside, almost explosively freeing herself of all her pain and frustration, she hardened her mouth as he had, and they took refuge in savage kisses which fuelled their fire, till neither of them knew what they were doing, only that they couldn't get enough of each other's lips, nor could they ever be too close.

Flesh to flesh, bone to bone, they sought mindlessly for unity. Frantic, breathless, Tiffany clung to Hassan, her wilful hands gripping his shoulders as his mouth swept masterfully over every inch of her face and down over her throat, and to the hollow at its base. There it lingered, moistly, and he became ominously still.

'Now we know,' he said thickly. 'Now we know, Tiffany.'

CHAPTER FIVE

TIFFANY'S humiliation was complete when she heard the quiet, exultant note in his voice. Hatred surged up to rescue her and she gathered the threads of control. Her self-respect was non-existent. She had to find it or be in his power. Her head went up.

'You can't tell anything from what has just happened,' she said scornfully. 'Have you ever considered that I might be using you? Maybe it was a test of my own power to arouse you, to see how much I could use my own sexuality to dominate *you*.'

Hassan winced noticeably. 'You bitch!' he seethed, his eyes flickering with lethal fire. 'You vicious little slut!'

'I feel no compunction about the way I behave towards a man like you,' she said coldly. 'I'll use any means I can, to win. And if you do force me to marry you, then you'll never be sure whether I'm responding to you or faking. You know what I felt about my late husband. One can't help but make comparisons.'

'My God!' he muttered thickly.

'I said, Sheikh Hassan,' she added tightly, 'that I could swallow all pride if necessary. That includes letting a man I despise make love to me.'

Straining her eyes in the black night, she thought his face looked racked with pain. But it was probably only a grimace of frustration that made his teeth flash like that.

'You wanted me——' he said hoarsely.

'Do you really imagine,' she asked in contempt, 'that I could want the man who has treated me so cruelly?'

'If I can hate and . . . want, so can you,' he muttered. 'They are close emotions. They can be mistaken for each other.'

'I'm not as hot-blooded as you. I think we established that early on. I certainly don't have your animal appetite,' she said scathingly, knowing with despair that what she said was untrue. It seemed she had, and it was a discovery that appalled her. She'd enjoyed everything he'd done, his touch, his passion . . .

Hassan's mouth twisted in a wry, mirthless smile. 'I'll saddle my horse,' he said abruptly.

Tiffany felt all the breath leave her body. She was safe. Her scorn had beaten him again. She felt limp from the effort.

When they moved on, into the heady, scented desert night, he walked alongside her, his head close to her thigh. He navigated by the stars, taking them over the cold sands, the swish of the horse's tail and the soft fall of shifting grains the only sound that broke the stillness.

Guilt at her response to him swept over her in flooding waves of embarrassment. She thought of her future and of spending each night of her life in his arms and was startled at the intensity of her excitement. It shouldn't be like that! She shivered and his eyes glinted at her. She could do nothing without his knowing. He was beginning to see into her soul.

To the east, the sun had crept over the horizon. For a magical few seconds, the sky was awash with pink light. Then it turned a bright cloudless blue.

Ahead were high dunes which rose like the softly rounded breasts of a woman's body. Swirling sand drifted from their peaks in small feathery gusts. As the horse moved into the sharp black shadow of a dune, she raised her face to the welcome breeze.

'Not long,' said Hassan quietly.

She thought his face looked different, despite the dark shadowing beard. Softer. Perhaps because their journey was nearly over. The future was daunting.

'Your new world. Your new life,' he said suddenly.

She looked at him in surprise.

'I suppose so,' she said heavily. 'I dread it. It'll be a living death.'

His mouth hardened and he made no comment.

'You—you'll be kind to Josef, won't you?' she ventured.

'He is my brother's son,' he said enigmatically, and she didn't push him any more, seeing he didn't want to talk to her.

Beyond the plain they were crossing, where the air danced with heat, lay a lush green valley. It was backed by a gigantic wall of jagged peaks.

'Tawi Atair,' said Hassan curtly, pointing to a faint irregular hill hanging behind a curtain of hot air. 'The Well of Birds.'

'Birds?' she asked in surprise, recalling that he'd told Josef something of this place.

He shrugged. 'Bee-eaters, purple sunbirds, hawks, magpies, herons——'

'Herons? There's a lake?'

Perhaps his home wouldn't be as harsh and unwelcoming as she had imagined.

'Thirty fathoms deep. Formed, so legend has it, by a falling star,' he said in clipped, flat tones.

In any other circumstances, she would have been delighted with the legend—and her surroundings. But fear nestled destructively within her body and she was in no mood for enjoying Hassan's country. Its pleasantness only served to emphasise her own desolation.

Gradually the hill turned into a huge fort looking as if it grew from a plug of rock, a sand-coloured castle, as in a fairy-tale. It soared into the air, flaunting its Crusader battlements, narrow window embrasures and huge ornamented arches. Tiffany saw it as a prison.

The tall towers rose over a hundred feet above a sea of palm groves, and surrounding those, like darkly moving waves, were fields of lucerne and indigo, spreading out in a challenge to the yellow desert. Tawi Atair was obviously self-contained; an island in a sandy sea.

Her eyes lit on a small dusty landing-strip, where two tiny planes gleamed in the sunlight. She must remember that. Maybe there would be a pilot who would fly her and Josef out, one day.

'Don't consider it,' murmured Hassan.

She flicked him a swift glance, hating the way he read her mind. It felt invasive.

'Oh, you're going to be wondering all the time,' she said, taunting him in defence. 'Wondering whether I've sold my body to this man or that, perhaps to a lorry driver, or a pilot. After all, we both know that I'm a cheap whore. I could easily seduce my way out of here, Hassan, and you'll never rest when we're apart.'

'That's why I intend to teach you such a thorough lesson in bed,' he snarled, 'that you'll have nothing left for any other man.'

'Impossible,' she said haughtily.

'We'll see,' he threatened.

Tiffany's face grew taut with strain. Hassan meant to rid himself of all his anger and sexual frustration on her. It would be a terrible revenge on an innocent woman. She *had to* persuade him that Nazim had ill-treated her and that violence would never win her over. Her stupid attempt to hurt Hassan by sarcastically suggesting she would sleep her way to freedom had back-fired on her. Damn! He won every time.

She tried not to slump in the saddle, though she desperately wanted to. Discipline kept her body upright. The years of pushing herself through the pain barrier to dance, to hold herself erect and graceful, were paying off again.

The white stallion walked through a line of frankincense bushes, their needle-thin leaves springing straight from contorted branches. Sap oozed from them, dropping into pots and filling the air with an exotic perfume.

And Tiffany's face softened a little when she saw the wild flowers beside the track. There were pansies, celandine and violets. It was almost like being home in England. Home! She gave a low moan.

'Josef!' she muttered. 'You said I could ring him——'

'At noon.'

'It's a long time to wait,' she said, defeated. Disappointment filled her face. Almost six hours. What could happen in those hours?

'We'll fill that time,' he said grimly.

She stiffened. He intended to slowly torment her with the hold he had over her. She'd fight every inch of the way.

'How far are we from other settlements?' she asked in a low voice.

'About a hundred miles,' he answered laconically. 'Don't think of running away. You'll never make it. The nearest town is far to the east, across the desert over there.'

He waved an arm vaguely towards some distant hills. There was no road, no track, only open desert. Tawi Atair was perfect for his abduction. Tiffany frowned. If she spent the rest of her life here, she'd go mad from the isolation. No wonder he behaved in such an extraordinarily arrogant way, if he was used to lording it over the locals in his own little world.

The massive iron-studded door of the fortress swung open and the stallion's hoofs clattered over ancient cobbles. Smiling-faced servants in white robes ran to greet them, and Tiffany looked for obsequious, fawning servility, but saw only friendliness and what appeared to be an easy relationship between them and Hassan.

Their smiles extended to welcome her and she found herself being swept along by Hassan and his chattering servants through a lush garden past hibiscus, daisies and camomile, beneath shading acacia, olives, and juniper. Its beauty was all the more poignant to the weary, apprehensive Tiffany. It ought to have been hard, ugly and uncompromising, to fit in with her situation.

In a small turret-room, at the top of a spiral staircase, the servants finally left her alone with Hassan. A wave of subtle perfume tantalised her nostrils as they entered, and she cringed at the thought that another woman, perhaps Hassan's last mistress, had inhabited these rooms. She shut her eyes to the wonderfully exuberant impact of the architecture and fabrics in the room and spoke before he got any ideas.

'I want a bath and a sleep and something to eat,' she said coldly, with as much authority as she could muster.

He threw her a mocking look and sat on a sumptuous divan, easing off his boots, dropping them on the soft oriental carpet and looking thoroughly at home. She didn't like the implications of that at all.

'Help yourself. That's a bathroom over there.'

He nodded towards a carved wooden screen between pale peach-coloured curtains which softened the honey stone walls.

She hesitated.

'There is a lock on the door,' he said sardonically.

'I should hope so. I want my own clothes back. I hate these second-hand, ethnic things.'

'I don't think Faridah would like to hear you describe them in that derogatory tone of voice,' he retorted. 'One of my cousins,' he continued, when she opened her mouth to ask whom he meant. 'She works for me here.'

'In this house?' she asked in surprise.

'Oh, she doesn't sleep here. She comes here every morning. We always have a working breakfast together. She's my public relations officer. Faridah usually goes home for dinner. Would that bother you, Tiffany?' he asked, his gaze sliding insultingly over her, his lips arched in a wicked smile within the black ruffian's beard.

'I'm not interested in anything but Josef and his safety. My mind is dead to everything else—particularly our relationship. Do what you like with me. After Nazim, no man will ever be able to earn my love,' she answered, with a challenging look.

His eyes flinched and she felt she was constantly scoring victories now. He was scowling at her comparison of him to his brother. Her confidence increased.

'I think you ought to make arrangements for your cousin to stay,' she said boldly, using his own sense of honour against him. 'Your servants will gossip otherwise. Do you want everyone to think your future wife is not to be respected?'

'I intended to ask Faridah to stay,' he said shortly. 'Even if you and I know what your reputation is, to the outside world it must be as if you are above suspicion. But I don't want you to mention our...arrangement. Not to her, or to anyone.'

'Why not? Is this some kind of trick?' she asked, her grey eyes alert. He couldn't be trusted, not one inch.

'I've said we'll marry, and we will,' he said in a low voice. 'But I think that for the time being people should imagine you're here of your own free will, as the woman who's working on a project of mine. I want them to think that we've decided your son should come here to join you.'

'You want me to act a part?' she asked incredulously. 'To pretend that I don't hate the very air you breathe?'

Hassan drew in a deep, angry breath. 'What will it do to my nephew if he arrives here, only to find that your hatred for me is public knowledge? How will he feel if gossip also tells him we are to be married? He'll be so confused he won't know what's going on. He'll be bewildered, incapable of handling the situation.'

He strode over to her and she backed away, wary of his barely leashed temper. But his long arm reached out and caught her shoulder, bringing her spinning towards him. She withstood the pain from his grip stoically, vowing that she'd die before she acknowledged he was hurting her.

'You have to pretend,' he snarled. 'As I will. Do you think I'll find it easy to show you any respect or courtesy? Everyone must think that we are falling in love gradually. If you love Josef, really love him, you'll make that sacrifice. He needs to get used to it here; to feel at home, before we drop any more bombshells on him.'

He was right, damn him! 'And if he doesn't like you? If he doesn't like it here at all?' she asked coldly, meeting his blazing black eyes fearlessly.

'That's one of the reasons we mustn't announce our arrangement too early,' he said grimly. 'I wouldn't keep him here against his will—it would be a waste of my time teaching him the business if he left the moment he could, as Nazim did.'

'Did Nazim hate you and your father, and this place so much, then?' she asked in a low tone.

Hassan's mouth thinned. 'Get this straight, Tiffany,' he said harshly. 'I don't want you to keep referring to my brother. He's dead.'

'If Josef doesn't want to stay, we wouldn't need to marry, would wc?' she asked, her throat tightening again at the thought of being his wife and lying in his bed every night, waiting for him.

He smiled nastily, encircling Tiffany with his arms, his hands pressing with arrogant possession into the small of her back so that she was forced against him. Their bodies met and Hassan's hot masculinity all but swamped her senses. She kept herself as rigid as a ramrod, and let herself shudder in disdain.

His hand shot up to her chin, making her look at him. 'You sly bitch! If I am given cause to think for one moment that you are turning Josef against me,' he hissed, his breath jerking out at her, hot and harsh, 'I will make you wish you were dead.' His eyes terrified her. She couldn't move for fear. Every word was bitten out in a savage fury. 'You agreed that Josef ought to have a chance—a fair chance—to see if he liked it here. You accepted that he should be given the opportunity to know his true inheritance. *Didn't you?*'

She nodded, incapable of speaking.

'And you accepted everything that went with that.' He shifted against her, the dark brooding of his smoky eyes flaring into a cruel desire as he deliberately branded her with the knowledge of his arousal. 'That includes warming my bed when and where and how I want. And how often I want,' he breathed.

Tiffany quailed and tried to shrink back from him. He wouldn't leave her alone, she could see that. She would be locked into a rerun of her soul-destroying marriage to Nazim. She'd stayed with *him* for Josef's sake, too, crushing her own loathing in order to bring her son up with some semblance of decency towards women, and with some morals. Oh, God! If only there were another way... Could she escape, so that he no longer had a hold over her?

If she did, then she'd have to take Jo from school and fly straight back to England; she wouldn't feel safe so near to Riyam. That meant disappointment for Josef—both in losing out on an uncle, and leaving his beloved school. Then there was her partnership with Charlie. She'd be letting him down. It was no use; the complications were too great. If she could, she'd stick out the marriage, providing Josef wanted to stay.

Hassan gave her an impatient shake. 'Pay attention to me!' he snarled. 'You have to allow my nephew to make a reasoned choice: comfort and a future here, or poverty with you. Not a choice based on your scheming lies and selfish hatred. Because that's what it would be, Tiffany,' he growled, his hand going to her hair and catching hold of a handful. Her head was pulled back and her vulnerable throat was exposed. 'So if you prove to me that you're totally selfish and are not truly concerned for Josef's future, I'll fling aside any remnants of civilisation within me and kick you out. But before I do, I'll destroy you. Physically, mentally, emotionally. You can be sure of that.'

'You vindictive bastard!' she muttered with difficulty. 'Let go of my hair!'

The hand, still on her back, now bent her into an arched bow so that he dominated her completely, his menacing face savagely dark as it leant over her.

'You will swear to be straight with Josef, and keep your opinions of me strictly to yourself. Let him make up his own mind, for his sake,' he growled.

'I swear!' she moaned, and he immediately let her up and released her. Desperately she sought for composure.

'I doubt,' she continued proudly, reaching up to arrange her hair again, 'that you'll be able to keep up the façade of being a charming uncle for long. Your foul temper will erupt and Josef will discover what a swine you are without any help from me.'

'You have nothing to worry about, then, have you?' he murmured.

'Nothing,' she said vehemently. 'You can't fool a child for long.'

'I'm banking on that,' he snapped. 'Now get yourself cleaned up. I want to shave and have some breakfast. Come down the turret stairs when you're ready. Here are your clothes.'

He began to stride out.

'Isn't this your apartment?' she asked with a frown.

She'd thought he had installed her here to be available for him, despite what he'd told her about his cousin.

'No. My mother's.'

'Oh, that's her perfume, then.' She sniffed the heady air.

'No. Mother died on the day I was born. The perfume is part of the walls. This was once a room in the women's quarters. When they were built, five hundred years ago, the clay was deliberately kneaded with the essential oils of flowers, instead of water.'

Tiffany's eyes widened at the sensuality of such an action. The very air she was breathing demanded her surrender.

'Was...?' She hesitated. 'Was your mother *loved*?'

Hassan frowned. 'Yes. By everyone who saw her.' He made to leave, and then added, 'I took her from Nazim by my very existence.'

Stunned by the emotion in his voice, she watched him leave, noting the raised shoulders and clenched fists. Both sons had been brought up without a woman's guidance.

That explained so much, suddenly. The cycle of deprivation mustn't be passed on to Josef.

Numbly, she went to the bathroom he'd indicated, locking the door and running a bath, clambering into the blissfully silky water. She stayed there a long time, thinking of nothing, blanking her mind. She'd take one hour at a time. It was the only way she could cope. And there were over five more of those hours before she could speak to Josef.

On a roof terrace looking over the Well of Birds, Tiffany sat down to an uneasy breakfast. Hassan had shaved and the pirate beard had given way to his smooth, infinitely touchable, golden skin. Once again, Tiffany was to marvel at his changing image and moods. For with the pale grey suit he appeared the epitome of the successful businessman, instead of the lawless desert barbarian. But she must remember that he was both of those, and more.

Faridah arrived, beautiful, with a rich flawless complexion and dark brown almond-shaped eyes. Her age was difficult to assess; she might be in her late twenties, or early thirties. Immediately Tiffany felt at a disadvantage in her crumpled cotton skirt and the simple jacket.

Tiffany had been introduced as Nazim's wife, so it was likely that Faridah knew what Hassan was up to. The woman was certainly hostile, and so probably knew Hassan's version of the facts.

Faridah's scrutiny had been unnerving.

'*This* is Tiffany?' she'd said, in a warm husky voice, her eyes sweeping contemptuously over the creased cotton. Faridah herself was wearing a cool Egyptian cotton suit, dazzling white, perfectly cut, and shaped beautifully around her curvaceous body. 'Hassan, she looks a little the worse for wear.'

Tiffany bristled at the venom-laced remark.

'I am,' she began grimly, intending to tell her why.

'Tiffany found the journey exhausting in the heat,' said Hassan smoothly, spooning up a dish of fresh strawberries, his dark eyes warning her.

'So I see,' said Faridah. 'Poor dear. You look *wrecked*.'

'Thank you,' said Tiffany politely. 'But I'll recover shortly. I will have regained my poise and my customary grooming when my luggage arrives. When might that be?' she asked Hassan with a faint smile.

Inside, beneath the cool mask, she wanted to throttle them both. Deception always made her feel guilty, and she had no idea whether or not she could pretend to like Hassan, let alone make sheep's eyes at him. Though it did give her a perverse pleasure to show him that she was in control of herself, and he wasn't crushing her as he'd imagined he might.

'Your things have arrived,' he said quietly, watching her carefully. 'They'll be in your room now. We wish to do everything to make you feel comfortable.'

Hypocrite! her eyes said to him. He seemed amused and sprinkled a little more sugar on his fruit, lifting a strawberry in his fingers and reaching across the table with it, so that it hovered an inch from her mouth.

'No, thank you,' she said pleasantly, with a false smile. 'If I eat that it'll bring me out in a rash. It would be like poison to me, you see.'

A lazy, mocking grin made him look wickedly seductive.

'I'll have it, Hassan,' said Faridah huskily, catching his wrist.

His lashes flicked down to her and his mouth lost its smile. Faridah dropped his wrist immediately, flushing. Tiffany stiffened. Even his cousin was afraid of him. She'd stepped over the line and he'd rebuked her with a mere movement of his eyes.

'You have your figure to think of,' he said suavely to Faridah. 'The strawberry is drenched in sugar. Besides, Tiffany isn't eating much, and after the desert ride she needs to eat. Particularly sugar, to give her energy.' He turned his dark eyes on Tiffany. 'You had little to eat on the journey. You mustn't make yourself...weak. That would never do, would it? We want you to be fit and strong.'

'I'm not weak,' she said firmly, realising, however, the truth of what he said and helping herself to a few slices of fresh pineapple. She did want to be strong, though not for the purpose he had in mind.

'You look washed out to me,' said Faridah languidly. 'I suppose Hassan only let you have a few meagre dates on the journey.' She looked sourly at Tiffany and her next words indicated that she didn't know how forcibly Tiffany had been abducted. 'I'm surprised you didn't object, travelling all that way with an unmarried male. If word gets out——'

'It won't, will it?' frowned Hassan. 'You and my driver are the only two people who know how far we travelled together. No one else will question my movements. Ahmed won't pass comment and I don't expect you to. Remember, Tiffany is my sister-in-law.'

'You shouldn't have spent the night out——'

'That's enough!' commanded Hassan sternly. 'You question my honour and Tiffany's, too.'

Faridah looked him up and down, her eyes betraying hunger. 'You are a man, Hassan,' she said softly. 'No one could deny the power that——'

'Faridah, I forbid you to speak of this any more,' he rapped, his face tense with anger. 'I'm going to start work. Join me when you've finished. Tiffany, I am not intending to burden you with my presence till you have rested after the journey. Make yourself at home. Sleep, wander around, borrow a costume from the clothes in your room and swim, if you wish. There are books in the library. I'll ring you in your room at noon.' His eyes glinted with a warning light. 'But I wouldn't step outside the confines of my house and gardens, though.'

'Why's that?' she asked brightly, deciding to test his reaction. 'I thought I might explore the oasis, perhaps take a brief camel ride into the desert while I was waiting for the hours to pass. I had a few camel rides in Turkey. They were fun.'

His hooded eyes hid what he was thinking, but Tiffany detected a slight twitching at the corner of his mouth.

'You have the stamina of an athlete,' he murmured.

'A dancer,' she corrected. 'That's what I was, before I had to give it up.'

'A dancer?' cried Faridah, with a look of distaste. 'That does explain a lot, doesn't it, Hassan?'

'Yes,' he said, his mouth twitching. 'It does.'

'Ballet dancer,' said Tiffany firmly. 'I had to forget everything but practice. We worked at something until we succeeded. We learnt never to consider failure, that the body—and mind—is capable of anything.'

'How interesting. It opens up all sorts of possibilities. It would be a shame to waste your talents on a camel. However, if you insist, I think it would be better to wait till I can be on hand to instruct you. I could give you a lesson and teach you the skills, if you like.' His tone had become husky. Tiffany knew that he was thinking of a more intimate teaching.

'I thought horses were your speciality,' she said icily.

He smiled. 'I'm very versatile.'

'Nazim was a good teacher,' she said, trying to sound wistful, and hoping Hassan would see the double meaning and leave her alone. 'A past master.'

A past master in demolishing her spirit, in subduing her with violence, she thought miserably. She must not let that happen again! Her eyes filled with unshed tears and she turned them on Hassan. The effect was astonishing. His sexual mockery was replaced by an icy rage.

Tight-jawed, and with a face of stone, he was having some difficulty in controlling his voice.

'Tiffany,' he growled, 'you are not to go out, for your own sake. You might stray a little too far—and then you wouldn't be able to ring Josef, would you?'

'What do you mean?' she asked, her heart thumping.

His whole body taut with menace, he laid a hand over hers, flattening it on the table.

'Only that you might lose all track of time and it will be too late to disturb him and take him away from his lessons,' he said, with a sinister light in his eyes. 'You wouldn't want to risk that, would you?'

He was bargaining with her. It was clear that she had to stay inside the fortress and behave herself, or she'd never be able to make that telephone call to Josef.

'I'll stay, as you suggest,' she said casually, then glanced down at her imprisoned hand. 'Don't you think you're being a little forward?' she reproved, in her best haughty English tone.

Faridah was seething. Tiffany felt uncomfortable about that.

'My concern for you made me forget my manners. Excuse me,' he said abruptly.

Tiffany watched him walk away, and realised wryly that Faridah was eyeing his broad back and tapering waist with open admiration. The woman's eyes were filled with desire and for a moment Tiffany felt sorry for her. Then felt worried for herself; Faridah would loathe her if she knew there was a marriage of convenience arranged.

'He makes my insides curl up,' breathed Faridah throatily, as Hassan's tall figure finally passed through the door at the far end of the terrace. Faridah fixed Tiffany with calculating eyes. 'And he's mine,' she said sharply.

Tiffany shrugged. 'You saw him first,' she said, assuming indifference. She'd have to talk to Hassan about this.

'I certainly did.' Faridah's hand banged down on the table. 'I belong to him!' she said fiercely. 'A female cousin always belongs to a male one! So keep off the grass. I have grazing rights.'

Tiffany bit her lip. She wanted to say that Faridah was welcome to them, but dared not. She'd promised she'd go through with this pretence and she was determined to keep her part of the bargain. And yet...

Joy flooded through her. If he and Faridah could get together, it would make all the difference; for surely, if he was married to *Faridah*, it would be all right for her to stay in his house, with a wife around. She brightened. Her own marriage to Hassan might not be a foregone conclusion after all! And yet, contrarily, she hated the idea of Hassan's marrying his cousin. It stuck in her throat to admit it, but she didn't want that at all.

'Watch him,' said Faridah, observing the changing expressions on Tiffany's lovely face through narrowed eyes. 'He's up to something.'

'Oh, yes?' enquired Tiffany, sipping her coffee with a studied air of casualness. Her heart began to thud. Faridah was thinking along the same lines as she was.

'Don't trust him. He's not being entirely honest about Josef.'

Tiffany stared, aghast. 'What do you mean by that?' she whispered hoarsely, every one of her senses jangling with alarm.

Faridah shrugged. 'It's perfectly clear to me. Hassan wouldn't spend most of his life and all his energy on the Sharif empire, only to hand it over to some kid, would he?'

'He has to leave it to someone——'

'You don't understand. When you've devoted your soul to something, as Hassan has, with a single-mindedness that's breathtaking, when you've let your personal life take second place, you won't rush to give it up. Besides, he'd lose the power and authority. He likes that.'

'Then why on earth did he seek Josef out?' puzzled Tiffany.

'My dear, you're very slow! Work it out. It's better to have potential trouble under your own roof. Hassan fears losing absolute control of his empire which he's built up so painstakingly. It's his whole life, Tiffany. Everything.'

Tiffany frowned. Faridah knew nothing of the arranged marriage. As far as she was concerned, Hassan was taking Josef into his house as a long-lost nephew.

'But Josef is just a child!' she cried. 'How can he be a threat? It'll be years before he can take over from Hassan——'

'Not years. Soon. When Josef is nine, he has the right to half the company because he is Nazim's son and it is his lawful inheritance. You, as his mother, will act for

him and Hassan will have to consult you on every move
he makes. That would be time-consuming and against
Hassan's belief that a company is more efficient with
one boss.'

'Surely Hassan knows that? Didn't he search for Josef
in order that he should inherit——?'

'He's probably thought of a way around the problem
of handing over half the company to a child in a year's
time. He'll have worked out some way to keep everything under his control,' said Faridah slyly, standing up.
'He wants total domination.'

Tiffany heard the echo of Hassan's voice and knew
the woman was speaking the truth. He went all out for
what he wanted.

'Ever since he was a child, Hassan has set himself impossibly high standards. And met them,' continued
Faridah. 'He's harsh with us all, but harsher on himself.
A man of great strength and of a great will-power. He
wants to be the boss. I don't think he'll gladly give up
half the company. To my mind, there's someone else
more deserving than your son. Do you honestly think
that a passionate and ruthless man would hesitate to trick
the child of his estranged brother and a whore?'

Tiffany's mouth opened in astonishment at the insult.
Her head whirled and she didn't even notice when
Faridah quietly rose and left her alone. Faridah had laid
her cards on the table; she resented the presence of a
potential rival and sought to undermine her. She'd succeeded in doing more than that.

Tiffany now knew why Hassan had been so keen to
marry her. As mere relatives, she and Jo would have
control over half of the Sharif empire. Marriage,
however, would bring them both under Hassan's control.
By becoming Josef's stepfather, Hassan would be able
to tell Josef what to do as far as the company was con-

cerned. As time went on, he could mould Josef to his image and only allow him a say in the running of the business if, and when, he wanted. No wonder Hassan looked so pleased with himself. No wonder he rode roughshod over any opposition she might put up. The stakes were very high.

And no wonder he insisted that she should pretend to fall in love with him, so that no one knew of his scheming.

Hassan was prepared to marry her for the sake of his rotten companies. What else might he do, to ensure no rival interference? Bound to her seat by the impossibly heavy weight of her own dread, she didn't run after Faridah and demand more information, nor did she move for several seconds. For within her was such a turmoil that it was all her body could cope with.

Hassan, she had to remember, was a particularly merciless man. He didn't behave like people she knew; out here there was a different law and it seemed he might be powerful enough to make his own. He had tricked her several times; deception came easily to him. Now he'd lured her into his den and she would have difficulty in escaping without being eaten alive.

Tiffany knew she had to play for time. Everything had happened so fast that she hadn't been able to chew things over. Somehow she had to put off Josef's visit without arousing Hassan's suspicion. And then she might have to manage her own flight, and face all the consequences.

She turned the matter over and over in her mind, trying to be level-headed, finding only confusion and panic instead. The garden beckoned, cool, calm, soothing. It might help her to sit there and think.

She had to play Hassan at his own game, but play a better one. If she could lull him into a lax frame of mind, she thought, slowly descending to the peaceful courtyard, she might convince him that there was a good reason why Josef shouldn't come just yet. Then she could find out a little more about Hassan and make a rational decision. She bit her lip. She'd have to be *nice* to him.

Could she do it? Could she butter up the man who intended to use her to his own ends?

Tiffany sat down and leaned her head against the stone wall, listening to the joyous bird song. It was ironic that here in this lovely garden she was so unhappy and that the peace only served to emphasise her chaotic thoughts.

A man's voice drifted through the window grille, close to her head. Instantly Tiffany tensed up inside, recognising Hassan's brusque tones. He was speaking in Arabic and seemed to be making a lot of curt arrangements. And then she heard a door slam and the sound of Hassan tapping out a long telephone number.

'Hassan al Sharif. Get me the legal officer, please,' he said. Tiffany lifted her head. Normally she would never listen to a telephone conversation. But this might be something to do with her. 'Marcia? I want you to do something for me, fast... yes, yes, I'm fine, and no, you're right, I don't waste time on preliminaries,' he said irritably. 'Listen, this is absolutely top priority. My US companies are to be handed over and I want you to start preparing the necessary paperwork. I'll no longer keep a managing interest...'

Tiffany's mouth opened in surprise. It was something to do with her, and Faridah was wrong! Hassan was already arranging to turn the companies over to Josef! A rush of relief hit her stomach in a warm glow. Whatever his attitude towards her, he did feel fond of his nephew. Thank God! She needn't worry about Josef's safety.

She heard Hassan talking again and tiptoed away, strolling into the beautiful building with its graceful arches and rich furnishings. Everything would be all right for Jo. She, well, that was another matter. She still needed *time*.

Tiffany went to her room, her mind a little calmer, but nevertheless pacing up and down restlessly, waiting, waiting, for the hour when she could ring Josef at school. Exhausted by the strain, she finally flung herself on the bed and slept a little more, wondering if she'd ever get back into some kind of routine. Hassan had turned her world upside-down.

He intended to do the same to Josef. What would her son think when he learnt that she intended to marry his uncle? She grimaced, knowing Jo would be thrilled, seeing it as some kind of fairy-story come true. For her, it would be a horror story, played in slow motion. When she was with Hassan it seemed that, although parts of her body raced out of control, it was as if she were living life at half-speed, every sense inflamed and intensified.

As the muezzin called the noon prayer, she had found her way to Hassan's study and was about to knock when he opened the door.

'Come in,' he said quietly. 'I was coming to find you.'

He stood aside and she swept past into a room lined with books, many of them antique. But there was nothing antique about the communications in this desert oasis. A bank of computers and machines, printers, photocopiers, fax, and a shredder were arrayed on a huge table running the length of the room.

'Give me the number and I'll get it,' he said.

'No, thank you. Give me the code and I'll do it myself,' she answered stubbornly.

He smiled, silent and watchful, assessing her in that calm, still way of his.

'Here.'

She turned the dial away from him so that he couldn't see what she was doing and rang the number, waiting while one of the masters went to find Josef, and his breathless voice answered.

'Mum? Is that you?'

Tiffany's eyes grew moist and a lump welled into her throat.

'Oh, Jo, hello, darling! It's wonderful to hear your voice! How are you? Everything all right?'

'Terrific! We had sausage and marmalade sandwiches, and when we went to bed we had a pillow fight. It was great. How are you? Is it nice there? I missed having a story...'

'I missed telling you one,' she said huskily, smiling fondly at his torrent of words. 'I'm fine.'

Tiffany looked up in alarm as Hassan picked up a phone.

'Hello, Josef,' he said in a warm, affectionate voice.

'Who's that?' asked Josef uncertainly.

'Hassan. Your uncle.'

'Oh, terrific! You there too? Are you keeping Mummy company?'

'Something like that,' he said, amused, his eyes lingering insolently on Tiffany's furiously quivering body.

'Jo,' she said, glaring at Hassan for interfering in her private call, 'have you got a match on Saturday?'

'Oh, Mum! I told you!'

Tiffany dropped her eyes. She'd known the answer to her question. It was all she could think of, to delay Josef's arrival here, till she'd thought things through. She needed to be certain of Hassan's intentions, and as yet she couldn't be certain he would treat her with some degree of respect.

'There's one on Wednesday afternoon here, and an away match on Saturday. I'm in the Colts, Uncle

Hassan,' he said eagerly. 'I wish you and Mummy could come over and see me play.'

'We will, one day, I promise,' said Hassan.

Tiffany seethed. Already they were a couple!

'Jo,' she said, 'your uncle was thinking that you might like to come and stay with him soon——'

'Oh, brilliant! Will you be there?' cried Josef enthusiastically.

Her heart raced and she was about to reply when Hassan interrupted.

'How about coming to my home on the next plane?' he asked smoothly.

'Wow! Will the job be finished then? Can Mum be there too?'

'Jo——'

'You could see the new pony I've bought, and come hawking with me in the desert,' continued Hassan relentlessly, challenging her with his eyes. 'Bring a costume, because we'll swim——'

'Oh, I'd love to,' said Josef, evidently torn, 'but you see, I mustn't let my team down. I'm the hooker, you see. That's awfully important. I'm bang in the middle of the scrum, and——'

'Josef, of course you must play your matches,' said Tiffany quickly. 'I wish I could be there. Perhaps, Uncle Hassan, I could pop back to watch the match?'

'Sadly, there's too much to do here,' he said, his eyes looking daggers at her. 'However, we could arrange for you to come after your Saturday match, Josef. Then you can tell me all about it.'

'Oh, yes,' cried Josef. 'I'd love a holiday. All the other boys have them but I've never had one.'

'I want you to come and see my home very much,' said Hassan in his velvet voice. 'I'll go and make arrangements for the flight now. After Saturday, then. I'll let you know the details. Will you be all right to travel alone, or——?'

'I'm used to moving around,' said Josef. 'I like flying. The airlines have got people who look after children my age. Oh, thank you! That would be great. Just great! I'm so excited, I could explode!'

'If you do, we could get your headmaster to parcel up the pieces and send you air freight, then,' joked Hassan.

Josef giggled and to Tiffany his laugh rang like a death knell. Her son was usually reserved, but he'd responded to Hassan with a natural and enthusiastic ease. Hassan said a fond goodbye to Josef and left her to continue the conversation alone, though her son wasn't interested in talking about school, only his forthcoming holiday and what they would do. Tiffany felt caught up in the web of deceit again: trying to pretend she liked Hassan and everything was fine.

It was painful ending the call. She missed Josef so much. Starved of love, she had poured all her passion into loving him. But soon she'd be with him again, one way or another. The first hurdle—preventing him from flying out immediately, as Hassan had wanted—was over. Next, in case she did want to run away, she had to gradually become familiar with the house and the surrounding countryside. Especially her escape route. Just in case.

On the roof terrace, she searched for the hills which Hassan had pointed out to her when they first arrived. Then she noted where the camel park was, and the airport, and imprinted it all on her mind. It was the first step. Next, she had to gain Hassan's confidence and make him trust her so that she could wander around Tawi Atair freely and learn the times of flights out, any daily lorry departures—anything she could glean which might help her plan.

It was a precautionary measure, one she hoped might never be needed. Perhaps she and Jo could make a good life out here. It all depended on Hassan.

And soon, she must suffer the ordeal of the evening, with Hassan making passes and Faridah hating her because he did so. Her only way out would be to bore everyone solid with motherly chat. She might be able to divert Hassan and get him to stop thinking of her as a woman.

Because she didn't want to think of herself as one. It was bad enough being cornered by Hassan in Oman. Here, where he had the potential to do whatever he wished, it was even more unsettling. Already he'd swept her into agreeing to marriage, and extracted from her a promise to give his outrageous plans a chance. What would be next?

CHAPTER SIX

LUNCH had been a solitary meal in the garden, and Tiffany longed for company, even Hassan's, to alleviate the monotony. The long, interminable afternoon was spent reading beneath the shade of palm trees there, and a kind of peace did finally descend on her, brought by the gentle warm breeze rustling the palm fronds, and the scent of herbs and roses drifting through the air.

Occasionally, a servant would wander out and ask if she wanted anything; coffee and cardamom, some halva, a dish of nuts, pastries, or fresh sherbet. There seemed no sense of haste in the servants' movements, and they took some pleasure in extending Tiffany's knowledge of Arabic.

Ideas began to crowd into her head, shapes, colours, fabrics, all for the leisure centre and all stimulated by the essentially oriental atmosphere around her. She missed working already. It would be infuriating never to work in the Middle East again because she'd had to run from Hassan's clutches.

Dinner was less of an ordeal than she'd expected. She'd wistfully eyed the bedouin garments in the wardrobe, and decided to stick firmly to her own clothes, putting on a neat green softly curving suit which would have won prizes for its modesty.

Faridah seemed subdued, as if Hassan had told her not to be rude, and he was in a good mood—probably because everything was going his way.

'You look better,' he commented, when she was shown into the dining-room.

'I did as you suggested, and relaxed,' she said pleasantly, looking around in awe. It was as if they were inside a vast bedouin tent, of pale gold silk, the sun filtering in through a glass roof and striking the circular brass tables beside richly embroidered ottomans.

'Please sit,' said Hassan, sinking gracefully on to the low seat.

His eyes travelled as if hypnotised up her long legs, and she felt the heat rise up her shins to her thighs as surely as if he'd slid his hand there. Her lips had fallen into a soft, treacherous pout and she wondered how much of his behaviour was for Faridah's benefit. He raised an eyebrow, and she tried to act as if she was just beginning to find him attractive. It wasn't difficult.

'I'm afraid I have the wrong outfit, for these low seats,' she said with a small laugh.

'Oh, I don't know,' murmured Hassan with a piratical grin, his eyes switching between her knees and Faridah's gold trousers.

'That's typical of a man's double standards,' said Faridah, with a smile she plainly didn't feel. 'You complain of the immodesty of some women and enjoy it at the same time.'

'I hope you're not suggesting that Tiffany is immodest?' he said mildly. 'I didn't give her the measurements of our seats and I presume she imagined we'd be eating western style. Besides,' he added, his dark eyes thoughtfully on Tiffany's face, 'a man does like some hints of a woman's attractions.'

'Clothes are important,' said Tiffany, trying to diffuse the undercurrent of resentment coming from Faridah. 'Particularly for me. I've been admiring your robe; is it traditional?' she asked, of his black sleeveless coat, edged with embroidery in gold thread. Its soft folds spread over his white tunic and trousers and she longed to feel the material.

'I forget,' he smiled. 'You're interested in cloth and design.' He shrugged it off, and passed it to her, making sure that he held on to it for a fraction too long so that they exchanged glances.

Tiffany hoped Faridah wouldn't be too hurt by what was going on. If she did decide to leave, it would only be a short pain. If she didn't, then it was best Faridah should have some inkling of what was to happen. As Hassan said, it made it easier for others if their 'romance' developed in public.

The meal was served, and Hassan took care to move closer to her and help her eat delicately with her fingers, his voice caressing, working its way into her senses. She found her body beginning to tingle every time he lifted his expressive hand, every time she became the object of his attention. He knew just how to appeal to her baser instincts, she thought resentfully.

'Tiffany,' he said smoothly, touching her shoulder, 'there are a few days till Josef comes, and Faridah and I have some business to do. Why don't you do some work in my office? Perhaps some preliminary sketches and notes.'

'For the leisure complex?' Her face had become elated. 'Well, I've had so many ideas since arriving here—I'd really like to be able to capture them.'

'If she's in your office, where will you work?' asked Faridah sullenly.

'There's enough room for the two of us,' he said calmly.

Both women shot him a suspicious look, but he seemed harmless. Tiffany's mouth quirked. Hassan would never be harmless.

'I'll hardly notice you're there. It occurred to me that you'd be bored, Tiffany, hanging around, waiting for the hours to pass,' said Hassan innocently. 'And it would be nice, getting to know one another like that, wouldn't it?'

'Yes,' she said warmly, letting her glance linger on him. 'It would be nice. Cosy.' She smiled brightly.

It was a good idea. She might learn a few things about his character. If he was worthy of being Jo's uncle, then the bizarre arrangement might work.

'Having said that,' mused Hassan, 'I need to call in to the souk tomorrow. Come with me, if you like.'

She did, and loved it, not worrying that his invitation had been an excuse to be seen with her in public. It didn't matter; she had his company and it turned out to be enormously pleasurable. She took her notebook, collecting samples of material from willing stallholders, making sketches and enjoying the chaos and noise, the hectic impression that she was in a tale of *The Thousand and One Nights*.

'Is Jo keen on markets like this?' asked Hassan, guiding her by the elbow and nodding in a friendly fashion at everyone they saw.

His changed manner astonished her. He was a different person—nice, warm, dangerously attractive. He'd reminded her beforehand that they must appear to be very friendly, because gossip travelled around the market like wildfire. So maybe it was the fact that she was responding to him as if he was very dear to her that made her feel weak at the knees. Her acting was even convincing herself!

'I could never take him in alone,' she said. 'I didn't like to risk it, not the kind of places we lived near.'

'No. Very wise. There are many times when you need a man, aren't there?' he said warmly, his hand briefly slipping up her arm in a blatant caress.

She stiffened, but he'd withdrawn his hand and was examining some carved wood, running his fingers lovingly over the flowers and leaves, his expression rapt. How sensual he was. He needed to touch. Nazim had just grabbed.

'What was your relationship with Nazim?' she asked suddenly.

Hassan started and threw her a dark look. 'He was my brother.'

'I meant how did you get on.'

'Don't all brothers quarrel?' he said lightly. 'Would you like some shoes made for you?'

'No, thank you. Did he resent you?'

'You have no right to pry into my past,' he said quietly.

'If we are to be married, I have every right,' she answered, a tremor betraying her nervousness about her future.

He walked her over to a low wall at the end of the market and brushed the whitewashed top for her to sit down. He placed a booted foot beside her and leant on his knee, staring at the green barley in the fields beyond. Water gushed down a small aqueduct below the wall, cooling the senses.

'We'll make it work, Tiffany. I promise you that,' he said in a low-pitched voice. 'My methods have been questionable, I know that, but they were for the best of purposes. And I think, now we've stopped fighting one another, our lives will be enriched.'

'By Jo,' she said quickly, hearing a compelling warmth creeping into his tone.

'Of course.' He smiled happily down at her. She had to smile back; he looked so delighted with life that it was catching. 'I had a long talk with him before we came out today.'

Her face became pained. 'You might have asked me if I'd like to speak to him——'

'I wanted to talk to him alone,' he said quietly. 'Be glad that I did. He worships you. I think I should forget the circumstantial evidence about your morals and look to the future. Jo and you and me. I'll be a good husband. I won't ever replace Nazim, I know that, but we do have a certain...rapport. Don't we?' He laughed, a little wickedly.

So that was the reason for his change of attitude. Jo had charmed him. The sun glinted on the hairs of his arm, turning them to threads of gold like the cloak he'd worn the night before. She had a terrifying urge to stroke his arm and feel the strength and the silky covering of hair.

'We ought to be getting back. You said you were busy,' she said hastily.

'So I did.'

He held out his hand to her in a gesture of friendship. Taking it, she felt his warm grasp and found herself wishing that he would never let her go. He drew her to him and she swayed pliantly in his arms.

'Is this real or are you faking?' he whispered.

'You told me how to act,' she said with a gulp. He must never know how strongly she was affected by him.

'Make it more convincing,' he said tightly, a glacial light appearing in his eyes.

So it wasn't real for him, she thought sadly. Just as well.

Yet for the next two days they worked in a companionable harmony. Tiffany became very engrossed in working on her ideas and found colour and pattern blending effortlessly within her head. She longed to get started in earnest.

Being with him was an eye-opener. Maybe he was working hard to impress her with his courtesy and business flair, but it did seem to come naturally. He was hard but fair. Her respect for him grew.

And there was the Majlis.

'I'm holding an audience,' he said, late in the afternoon of the second day. 'Come and see it. I think you'll be interested.'

'You're doing a variety act?' she asked flippantly, to disguise the rush of warmth at his eagerness to include her.

'As sheikh of a thousand tents in this area, I am bound to make myself available for minor official acts,' he said, pride bringing an offended reserve to his face. 'Don't make fun of an ancient custom.'

Tiffany walked with him along marble corridors towards the largest salon, thinking about this.

'Will Josef inherit the title of sheikh?' she asked, trying to imagine her son as lord of a thousand tents.

'Only if he deserves it. It's not a hereditary title. You have to earn it.'

'How?' Tiffany felt pleased. That counted for something, didn't it? Hassan's character must be special for him to have been chosen.

He shrugged. 'Courage, generosity and mediating skill.'

'Oh.'

He smiled to himself at her contemplative face and motioned her to a seat where she was hardly visible. For the next two hours, people of all descriptions and all walks of life came to Hassan for his help. She knew nothing of what they said, but later he explained that he'd settled water disputes, arranged pipeline rents,

grazing rights and oil concessions, and patched up griev-
ances. And Tiffany could see how well he listened and
that everyone looked up to him. It wasn't an act for her
benefit and she felt the tug of ungovernable longing and
admiration mingle with hope.

That evening, he came closer and touched her more
boldly, speaking to her gently, smiling, heating the very
air with his evident sexual attraction, bombarding her
senses till she could hardly think straight. Of course, she
was forced to play along. Forced? She had to admit that
she was more than enthusiastic. Not many men aroused
her admiration. She smiled wryly. She found him
irresistible.

Every hour that passed, she fell more and more under
his spell. She began to give in to her feelings, knowing
with a sense of excitement that they could have an incredible relationship. For his part, it was clear that his
antagonism and contempt had gone, and for Josef's sake
he was burying the hatchet he'd wielded against her.

Despite her nagging uncertainty about Josef's well-
being, and the fact that she missed him and looked
forward to her long chats with him, she also looked
forward to the days cloistered with Hassan in the big,
cool office, revelling in his comments on her work with
an almost childishly glowing pride.

Even more, the bittersweet moments when they pretended to be falling in love brought her equal measures
of joy and pain. She almost believed that the sensual
crescendo he was working towards flowed naturally from
him, and wasn't part of a calculated plan. His affection
seemed too real. It made her yearn to trust him and to
give in to her instinctive longing to release her suppressed love. But she dared not, yet.

It was just as well. For, one morning when they were in the study together, there came a fatal telephone call and Hassan walked innocently into his own snare.

'Hassan here...New York? Put them on... Morning, Marcia! You've worked fast... What about the US holdings...? Oh, the new owner! Didn't I say? His name is Abdul al Sharif.'

In a split second, Tiffany's warm glow turned to a hard, cold lump of nausea, clawing at the pit of her insides. Looking down on her shaking hands, she listened on in consternation.

'Bring the papers over yourself immediately. The matter must be completed by that date I gave you... Fine. See you then.'

The receiver dropped down and Hassan continued with his work, whistling cheerfully under his breath. Tiffany sat numbed with shock. She didn't know whether to say anything or not. It dawned on her that he didn't know she'd heard his earlier conversation with Marcia and would therefore be able to put two and two together.

It added up to disinheritance, of course; Hassan was shedding ownership of companies so that they weren't under his name any longer. In the event of her marriage not going through, Josef could never claim them, because they would no longer be owned by Hassan. But why give up ownership? Wasn't Hassan sure of his hold over her?

There would have to be another reason, a strong one, for him to hand over something he valued so much. Abdul al Sharif. The same surname. Who could be so important...? Her hand leapt to her mouth, as she realised the full implications. There was no other possibility. Abdul must be the person Faridah had referred to when she'd said there was someone more deserving of the inheritance. Hassan wouldn't hand his beloved business over lightly, not to anyone. This person would be someone very close, if he was to be given the US companies.

She considered the possibility which had sprung into her mind. Hassan would hardly have led the life of a monk. One of his women might have produced a child. For to whom else but a bastard son would he transfer his precious companies?

And if Abdul was older than Josef, that might be another reason why he'd been so all-fired eager to marry her; the *elder* son would inherit the whole Sharif empire, not a mere stepson. Jo would have nothing.

Whereas he did have a strong claim at the moment, as Nazim's child, and that was probably why Hassan was taking precautionary measures to safeguard his bastard son's future, transferring some of the companies before Jo took his rightful share.

Tiffany's mouth tightened. That scheming, devious, sly swine!

She passed a weary hand over her forehead. The situation had changed. Hassan wasn't to be trusted to do the best for her son. The sooner she and Josef got out of his clutches, the better.

Her eyes glittered. She wanted to confront Hassan, to have a blazing and satisfying row. But she dared not say anything. Her plan must be to allay his suspicions. Otherwise he'd put a guard on her and she'd never escape.

Misery filled her heart. The last two days had been enjoyable. Even...special.

'Tiffany?'

She jumped. Hassan's hand had descended on to her shoulder.

'What is it?' she said, trying to smile.

'You've been dreaming for the past minute or two. And I see you've been doodling with your pencil all over your design for the powder-rooms.'

She looked down in consternation.

'Oh! How stupid of me! I was wondering about the fabric for the curtains.'

'Were you?'

Nodding brightly, she tipped her head on one side, as if still thinking. But Hassan twirled her chair around and tilted up her chin.

'You find it hard to put aside your feelings for Nazim?' he queried. 'Won't you let me help you get over him?'

His eyes dropped to her mouth and she felt his breath rasp a little more harshly. It was unbearable having him so close. Every one of her nerves screamed to be set free by him, from him—she didn't know what she wanted, only that he disturbed her more than any man ought to. Especially a clever, manipulating one who pretended to be charming in order to hide his convoluted plans.

His fingers slid smoothly over the hollow below her cheekbone and along her jaw. There was a fierce message in his eyes; one of tenderness and love, of burning desire. And she was caught up in it, unwillingly, incapable of dragging her gaze from his, incapable of preventing her face from flushing with warmth.

If he'd done this one hour ago, she would have responded differently. He was too late.

With a reluctant effort, she reached up and held his hand, meaning to remove it, but he plundered it with kisses and it was all she could do to prevent herself from crying out in despair.

'A couple of days can make all the difference between love and hate, can't it?' he mused, with a winning smile.

She wasn't won. Her heart had to be hardened against his easy charm and effortless sex appeal.

'All the difference,' she said wryly, seeing the irony of his words. An hour ago, she was falling in love. Now she wasn't. Simple. 'I think I'll go up now,' she said. 'I want to wash my hair and so on before dinner.'

'There's only the two of us tonight,' he said huskily. 'You don't have to be so modest in what you wear. Put on something . . . gorgeous for me. Please.'

She pushed him away with a light laugh.

'I would have thought that was just the occasion *not* to wear anything that didn't button up to the neck,' she said, managing to grin convincingly.

'I haven't attacked you, or treated you badly,' he said with a slight frown. 'Please. To prove you trust me. And for me to prove I can admire and sit on my hands at the same time,' he added with a rueful grin.

She tried to sound normal. Flirt! she told herself.

'Not all the time, I hope,' she smiled, trying to look provocative.

Hassan drew in his breath. 'Do you need any help to change?' he asked huskily.

Faridah saved her, by walking in on them.

'You won't be much use to me,' grinned Tiffany with a supreme effort. 'Not if you're sitting on your hands. See you at dinner,' she finished with a light laugh.

Outside, she let her body slump with fatigue. But the battle wasn't over. The worst was to come. As she toiled unhappily up the stairs, she concentrated on working out her actions for the next few hours. It was Thursday already and she had to find a way to get out of Tawi Atair. He must feel certain of her devotion, even if it meant she had to let him ogle her all evening. For Josef's sake, it was essential that Hassan never suspected what was in her mind. And then she'd find a means of fending him off after dinner. She had to.

Already her stomach seemed full of butterflies at the prospect of striking the right balance between enticing Hassan and perhaps inviting her own rape, and offending him with her reserve. Not easy. For that, she'd need an elegant outfit and a cool head—and perhaps a well of scorn, ready to pour on him if he ventured too far.

Hassan was nobody's fool, and he might just take what she offered, without caring about her feelings at all. Still, it was all she could think of to put him off the idea that she might be secretly plotting to get away.

Slipping into a satiny bra and briefs, she dragged her clothes out and laid them on the bed. Naturally she had been expecting to be working in Oman, and had brought one or two elegant items for the evening.

Not the black sheath. Although it had a bolero jacket, Hassan had X-ray eyes and impertinent fingers. She couldn't risk his discovering that beneath the jacket the apparently demure dress had a boned, strapless top which revealed a great deal of her breasts. It would have to be the cinnamon suit, she decided. It struck the right note between sophistication and allure, with its deep V neckline—which could be buttoned high or low—the cinched-in waist, and the hip-hugging skirt.

She put away the rest of her clothes and did her face carefully, enlarging her soft mouth deliberately and enhancing her eyes with soft grey shadow. It was still very warm, and she decided to dispense with her new bra and wear a thin camisole top instead. It was halfway over her head when it caught on a loose link of the safety chain on her watch.

And that was when Hassan chose to knock on her unlocked door.

'Tiffany?'

She struggled furiously with the top, her arms trapped and her head in its folds.

'Tiffany!' he called again.

'Hassan! Don't come in!' she called out in a muffled voice.

To her horror, the door opened. She froze in shock. There was a silence. All she could see was his shiny black shoes, but the atmosphere had heated more than a few degrees. She wriggled, hoping the camisole would free itself, stupidly not thinking of the obvious solution to her over-exposure.

'Later, Hassan,' she called in cool amusement, remembering not to antagonise him. She regained her senses and turned her back on him. Her throat was dry from nerves as she tried desperately to free herself in the deafening silence.

'Later? Any reason why not now?'

Tiffany was more caught up in the camisole than ever. And in her own deceit, dammit!

'I thought you enjoyed waiting,' she said in a muffled voice, feeling hot and uncomfortable, knowing he must be staring at her naked back and enjoying the way she wriggled. 'You said that could be exciting.'

'Well, well, well. Faridah was right about you after all. Trust a woman not to be fooled,' murmured Hassan. The door slammed. 'You make a very enticing sight.'

'No——!'

'Tiffany,' he said huskily, 'I'm not made of stone. You can't expect me to turn down an offer like this.'

'Oh! It wasn't an offer! Oh, damn this top——'

'Let me help. You seem to be badly tangled up there.'

'Go away,' she said mutinously, abandoning her attempt at coaxing him to leave. 'I can do it.'

'But I want to,' he husked. 'I can't stand the distance between us, nor stop my hands from touching your skin.'

She gasped as she felt his hands boldly cup her naked breasts and then he had pulled her hard against his rapidly breathing chest, the whole of her back burning from the heat of his body.

'Beautiful, beautiful,' he crooned into her ear.

The relentless movement of his hands made her groan aloud in rage, and then she had torn her top free and was trying to settle it down on her body. It dropped to cover her a little, but his mouth savaged her neck, hungrily sweeping it with passionate kisses, increasing the ache within her as his freely roaming hands explored her curves.

'Let me go, Hassan!' she said huskily.

'No,' he growled. 'You can't tease me and get away with it. You knew exactly what you were doing, didn't you?'

'No, I didn't! And you know how I feel——'

'Hell! I'll make you forget!'

He spun her around and his mouth drove into hers, savage, hating, and they were locked as if in combat, an elemental rage hurting them both. She tore her mouth away.

'Hassan, what has Faridah been saying?'

'That you're a tease. That your coolness is callousness. That you bet her you'd bring me to my knees with wanting.'

'No!' she cried in horror. 'She's lying! She wants you for herself——'

'You bitch!' he growled. 'That's a lie. I know who she mopes over and it's not me. You're trying to wriggle out of the truth. You enjoy throwing out your body as bait to helpless men, don't you?'

'Helpless?' she cried incredulously. 'You're about as helpless as a wolf in a sheepfold.'

'I should have kept faith with my brother's word, with Faridah's, with my investigator's, with the evidence of my own eyes,' he snarled. 'Not let myself be duped by you and your poor, innocent son. There's a name for women like you,' he breathed, his eyes impaling her with their venom. 'You've probably left a trail of broken men, haven't you? You certainly spoiled my brother's chances of ever making anything of himself. So...'

She gasped as he thrust her down on to the bed, his teeth tugging urgently at her bottom lip, and as she cried in protest his tongue slipped into her mouth with an unbearably erotic movement, inflaming their mutual need.

She seemed to be swamped in sensation. There was a hand curving, stroking, over her velvet hip; fingers shifting with intoxicating halting movements beneath the silky camisole, around the curve of her breast; Hassan's mouth filling hers with sweet hunger; his groans and his breathing, his muted growls, eloquently tormenting her sense of hearing; and his eyes, his damnable eyes, scorching, searing into her brain till it dissolved into mindlessness.

His plundering mouth moved relentlessly, savouring, gentling now, less voracious, but no satisfactory substitute for the act she longed for. And she felt the heat of his body and the dangerous power that lay so hard upon her with a sinful thrill of pleasure.

'No, you can't——'

'I damn well can!' he breathed.

His hands had roamed to her bare shoulders, revelling in the buttermilk softness, his lips following them, across her throat, her collarbone——

'No, Hassan!' she cried, her voice raw with need. He had aroused her so easily that she could have wept with shame.

'Yes,' he said hoarsely. 'I will. I will have you. You're not a young virgin. You enjoy sex. And,' he growled, 'you can't deny that you invited me in, knowing how naked you were. I only came up to ask if you'd like to eat out. Now, I suggest, I eat in. Here...and...here...and here, here, here...'

Tiffany moaned at the exquisite demand of his mouth. 'I didn't——'

'I'm not going to argue. I am here and here I stay. Till I have what I want. Unfortunately,' he said, insolently cupping her breast and rubbing it with an intolerable rhythm of his palm, 'you won't be able to twist me around your little finger. I will be the dominating one in our relationship.'

'Dinner——'

'Is served up on a plate,' he mocked. 'A little earlier than expected.' His hands ripped away her bodice completely.

He shuddered as her naked body was totally exposed to his lusting eyes. Tiffany's hands reached up to thrust him away, but he effortlessly caught her wrists and she was only able to writhe helplessly beneath him as he drank his fill.

'You are very, very lovely,' he breathed harshly.

One wondering mouth dropped to a taut dark peak and her anger and fear were swept away by the agonising sharp pains of exquisite need which rocked her body. He was making her head spin; she was out of control, only able to concentrate on his devouring mouth as it captured each hard rosy centre, savouring hungrily, creating an impossible emptiness within her.

'You bastard!' she moaned, arching her supple back.

He grunted deep in his throat and she felt the hard ridge of his hip shift slightly. The tugging on her breasts softened, deepened, became more impassioned, and she could stand his tender, expert loving no longer. Small moans erupted from her lips, her head turned from side to side, and she became aware that Hassan's lips were drifting upwards, sliding over her skin, to her jaw, her lips, sweetly moving in a trail of soft fire.

'I—I—can't bear this,' she jerked haltingly. 'Please don't. I beg you.'

'I want you,' he muttered. 'And as long as there is breath in my body, I intend to make sure I take you, and see if you're worth all my desire. I have to know. We both have to know.'

'I don't understand!' She shuddered as his hands slid up the length of her thigh.

And she was encouraging him, amazingly, hopelessly, conniving in her own ruin, as he slid his savouring hands over her thighs, edging his knees between them. Tiffany squirmed as the sweet moistness within her signalled its unmistakable message, the wanton voluptuousness of her sinuous body making his mouth arch in carnal curves.

'Hassan!' she urged, closing her eyes so that she couldn't see what she was allowing. But she could feel. Oh, she could feel—a hotly inciting movement of his fingers, which scattered her senses to the four winds.

'Tiffany. God, we create fire between us!'

His mouth grazed her shoulder, savaged her nipples with brutal tenderness, and then she felt his tongue slicking around the curves of her breast in a light touch so delicate that she kept straining towards it.

The raw emotion within her and the pure, physical response were new. It was frightening. She had no idea that her body could take over so completely and deny her mind, nor that a man could be so gentle and so infinitely desirable because of that. She fought for consciousness, but Hassan's lovemaking was too passionate to allow that to surface.

There was only her dark need.

'Kiss me,' he murmured. 'Kiss me, Tiffany. I want you to. Hard. With all your passion, all your desire. Tell me what you want. How you like it.'

She gloried in him. Her treacherous mouth rose to his, her starving lips lush and full in expectation.

The telephone rang.

The lifting of Hassan's body from her, and the sudden cool air on her breasts came as a cold shock—and a terrible loss. One of his hands had remained on her breast, teasing it, exploring, enticing. She gave a sharp, involuntary moan and his eyes melted into hers.

'Yes?'

Tiffany blinked, her racing pulses making the blood roar in her head, as Hassan answered the phone.

'In a minute.'

He slammed the receiver down and for a moment was silent, his chest heaving with ragged breath. Then his storm-laden eyes turned to her and ran slowly over her body, leaving shock-waves in their path. Unconsciously, she lifted her body a little, desperate for his touch.

Hassan's breath exhaled noisily.

'I daren't touch you,' he said harshly, as if he knew what she wanted by a mutual sexual instinct. 'Not now. I hadn't meant . . .' His white teeth ground into his lower lip. 'Hell!' He stood up shakily. 'You make me lose all self-control! Well, at least there will be something to enjoy in our marriage,' he said cruelly.

Tiffany's eyes widened and she felt a stab of fierce despair. She had made herself cheap and he felt fully entitled to treat her like a slut. She lay there and tried to tell herself that it didn't matter. Soon, very soon, she would be out of his reach.

'Faridah has been trying to get hold of me,' he said, sounding husky. 'She's very angry that she found me here, I think.'

Tiffany groaned. 'You bastard,' she said in a flat tone.

He leaned over her and she shrank into the mattress.

'Hate me?' he queried, his eyes glittering.

'You know I do!' she breathed with venom.

He laughed and bent his head to her breast, feeding greedily, and her hands automatically went to his shoulders, smoothing over their gold satin, her whole body alive once more.

'Want me?' he growled in his throat.

'No!' she quavered, her hips jerking with the intolerably tantalising movement of his fingers.

'No,' she said desperately, as he slid down her body, his shockingly intimate kiss breaking all her resolve in a blazing furnace of wanting.

'Oh, you devil, you devil. Yes,' she moaned, lifting her hips in response. 'Yes, damn you, damn you!'

'Yes?' he whispered, in a simmering voice, shaking with passion.

Tiffany whimpered, driven beyond endurance at the lightly feathering kisses, the moist heat of his mouth.

'Please,' she begged, unable to stand any more. '*Please*, Hassan!'

He moved up her body, his eyes holding her, quickly easing his tie and flinging it aside, removing his shirt, unlatching his belt... She gasped with anticipation, as his hands twined in her hair, his desire-laden eyes mesmerising her beneath the heavy lashes, and she fell into a spiralling whirlpool of emotion.

'We can't...'

'We must,' he breathed hoarsely.

She shuddered at the tantalising distance of his sultry mouth.

'Kiss me,' she moaned. 'For pity's sake...'

A gossamer touch brushed her lips.

'I hate you,' she sobbed with need.

'Hate, want, they seem to be one and the same thing for us,' he rasped.

Her hands were helping him to slide off his remaining clothes—hands that moved without any conscious will on her part. He shuddered as his body lay on hers and for the first time they were skin to skin, knowing every inch, every aching, longing inch.

'Oh, my darling,' he husked. 'You are wanton, beautiful...'

She felt a delirious sensation at his words and then he was drowning her in his kisses, with more passion than she'd ever known could exist.

'You've taken over my whole mind, my body. I can't think of anything but you, can't envisage life without you near me, enticing me. This is the only thing that's been on my mind for days,' he said harshly.

And suddenly he had lifted his hips and the hard, infinitely desirable heat against her loins drove into her with a sweet, welcome thrust. Deep within her, she felt her muscles begin to contract rhythmically in automatic response.

'Beautiful,' he croaked. 'Slow me down, Tiffany, oh, slow me down!'

'What?' she mumbled dazedly. 'How...? I don't...'

'God!'

His fingers caressed sublimely, taking her to the brink and beyond. They rolled on the bed and she matched his frenzy, scorching him with her kisses, their mouths murmuring, suckling, nibbling, biting...

And he moved. Moved like a gentle, slow piston, till she yelled for more and she demanded her own satisfaction from him. Their rhythm was perfect. He called her name hoarsely, in agony, and faster and faster he possessed her, flooding her with sensation after sensation, leading her to a terrifying crescendo of emotion which made her bury her head in his neck and sob with relief.

But instead of stopping, he moved delicately, marginally, subtly, while she moaned for him to stop, and then he twisted her around so that she sat astride him, her breasts dropping heavily in his hands, and new trickles of arousal were beating at her body, his mouth sliding seductively over every inch of her skin. Again, with a quickening hunger, he drove her to a climax, leaving her clutching blindly at him for support.

He laughed softly in exultation, falling back with her on the bed, stroking her gently, muttering soothingly as she sought to control her senses and breathe normally again.

But he turned her deftly on to her stomach and gently massaged her back and her buttocks until she was helplessly tormented, begging him to continue. Only when she had reached almost total physical and emotional exhaustion did he relent and then he finally released his own restrained virility.

'Watch me, Tiffany,' he said thickly, as his head dropped back in an intense sexual need. 'Watch me love you!'

It awed her. She watched him, every second of his pleasure, every subtle change in his face, as it became suffused with passion. She had never known she possessed such heightened senses. She felt the muscles in his pelvis and legs tense up, one by one. Every part of his body seemed to be throbbing, humming. Beneath her fingers, his shoulders bunched and flexed; her mouth lingered softly over each fine, curling hair on his chest. The look of pure, unadulterated ecstasy on his face tore at her heart, wrenching it open, as a sweet tenderness flooded through every vein she possessed.

It was a moment of miracles. Of a blinding, terrifying realisation that if this man only loved her, if he had one ounce of affection for her, she would love him until her dying day.

'Oh, Tiffany!' he groaned.

Slowly, very slowly, bewildered by the depth of her emotional response, she watched him return to sanity again. His body relaxed, muscle by muscle and now she knew every one of them.

They lay entwined, bathed in sweat, and he languorously licked her with his tongue, letting it rasp on her skin so that she shivered. Then he caught her in his arms and held her tightly as if he never wanted her to be separated from him.

'Tiffany,' he whispered, 'I make no apologies. We both needed each other. We were made to be bound together for all time. I've never made love like that before.'

She was too indolent to speak. He cradled her in his arms like a child and she nestled up, bemused and spent.

'I knew it would be like this,' he murmured, stroking the sun-gold of her hair. 'The moment I saw you. The moment your eyes flashed at me. And when I saw your body...' He kissed her forehead. 'It was inevitable, wasn't it?' he mused. 'That we should possess each other.'

Tiffany lay supine, letting him caress her lightly, her mind a blank, not daring to think, her body as still and her brain as emotionally battered as if it lay in the aftermath of a storm.

Mutely, she let him carry her to a rose-scented bath, and she shared it with him. He soaped her body, gently, tenderly, adoringly.

'Hassan——'

He stopped her mouth with a light kiss.

'Forgive me,' he said in a low voice. 'If I hurt you, if I frightened you, it was because I always knew how completely you would captivate me. I still feel anger for that. No one rules me, no one. I understand why Nazim had to love you.'

'He didn't,' she said, her tremulous mouth parted. 'Not in a normal way. Oh, Hassan!' she lifted her arms to him and he wrapped himself and then her in bath robes and led her back to the bedroom, lifting her shaking body on to the bed. She couldn't bear his gentleness.

'What is it?' he asked gruffly, cradling her in his arms. 'Do you still think you yearn for him? Or can you admit that at least you feel a powerful emotion for me?'

'I-I—desire you,' she said hesitantly.

'No. It's more than that,' he said fervently, murmuring against her hair. 'There's a deeper feeling, isn't there?' he coaxed. 'Admit it.'

'No,' she said, reluctant to accept that she felt anything more than a sexual attraction for him. Anything else was impossible.

'Something has drawn us together, overcome all our hate and gone beyond it. Whether we like it or not, you are my life's blood, Tiffany. And I am yours.'

'I don't want——'

'Neither do I,' he growled. 'But it's useless denying our feelings. Fate has tied us together, and we are helpless in its path.'

'How can I trust you?' she cried piteously. 'I want to believe——'

'We have just been honest with each other,' he said softly. 'Our bodies have told us what we will learn one day to be true. Giving yourself to someone makes you vulnerable, Tiffany. I don't lightly trust myself with a woman—not as I did with you. Believe that. The rest will come in time.'

Her soft grey eyes kindled at the gentleness in his face. Her heart wept in hope. Wordlessly, she lifted up her arms and he held her very tightly. When they parted, her eyes were filled with emotional tears.

'I can't,' she whispered. 'I daren't.'

'Can't ... love me?'

'Hassan—I don't know what to think. I——'

'Let your body and your heart speak,' he husked, kissing away her tears.

'I'm so confused,' she mumbled. 'There's something inside me I want to reach and I can't find it.'

'I know,' he said, in a choking rasp. *'I know.'*

They lay together, curled into one another, talking. Tiffany felt released from her defences, stunned that they could share confidences and dreams so easily. And even more surprised that Hassan seemed prepared to be patient, to wait until she felt secure and could trust him.

That wasn't yet. Soon she would have to start asking him to explain his actions about Abdul, and she was subconsciously putting off that moment. Her dreams might disappear like sifting sand.

'Are you hungry?' he asked softly.

She widened her eyes and opened her bruised mouth in alarm. But he laughed, his grin dazzling her and making her heart lurch.

'No, sweetheart,' he said. 'Later. I wondered if you wanted some dinner.'

She sat up in horror. 'Faridah! She rang——'

'Yes.' Hassan grinned at her disarmingly. 'I fear she'll be putting two and two together.'

'Oh, no!' moaned Tiffany, her body flushing a soft pink.

Hassan bent and kissed as much of it as he could reach, while she tried to push him away, grumbling gently.

'Don't worry,' he murmured. 'We'll just have to tell her straight away what has happened.'

'She'll be upset . . . She does love you.'

He laughed. 'No.'

'She does,' insisted Tiffany. 'That's why she's been wary of me ever since I arrived.'

'No. It's because you married the man she loved,' he said gently. 'Nazim. You won his heart.'

Tiffany was silent, wondering what to say. Faridah had lost Nazim, and now it must appear that she was about to lose Hassan too. All because of a blonde Englishwoman. It wasn't surprising that there was hate in Faridah's eyes. Had the woman deliberately misled her?

'This has changed everything, though,' continued Hassan softly, kissing Tiffany's nose. His lips brushed the full softness of her mouth and she trembled. 'We can't live together in this house for long without everyone finding out what we're doing each night. We must get Josef here immediately, and be married as fast as possible.'

She felt a chill settle within her. 'Don't rush me——'

His smile vanished. 'You agreed. Surely you must see we need to hurry the ceremony along? After all,' he said, his voice becoming agonisingly husky, 'you could already be carrying my child.'

CHAPTER SEVEN

TIFFANY felt the ice move down her spine. Their love-making had been so urgent, so impossible to stop, that she hadn't considered taking precautions, and neither had he.

And now he sounded so keen to get Josef into his power. How could she believe that he was being honest with her? What if he'd deliberately made love to her, so that she was bound to him—as she had been with Nazim? Oh, God! Had she led herself into a trap? Exactly the same one as his brother had laid for her? How could she be so stupid?

She had no reason to trust him, and every reason to be suspicious. Hassan now had what he wanted: her sexual submission. With that, he would soon manipulate the situation so that he also had Josef in the palm of his hand.

'It's all right, Tiffany,' Hassan was saying. 'I'll deal with Faridah. Don't shake like that. It'll be all right. I'll go down now and talk to her. I'll send up some supper for you, and be up later. I want to sleep with you, tonight,' he purred, his hands threading through her soft hair.

The sensually sweet brush of his mouth and hands induced a drowsy liquidity on her sensitised flesh, slow ripples of warmth making her shiver.

'I think I'd better go,' he said in a bemused voice. 'Before Faridah comes up here.'

'Hassan!' she said hoarsely, her eyes huge.

'Mmm?'

She struggled to sit up and he made a low, male growling sound in his throat.

'Go!' she pleaded.

He sighed and moved away, dressing quickly, her heart beating fast to see his superb body. She wanted to touch him, and when he turned he saw that and smiled, making her heart ache.

'Tell me you want me and then I'll go,' he said, in a voice harsh with tension.

The words hurtled out, wild and tormented. *'I want you!'* Oh, she moaned inside, the unfairness of it all!

'Yes,' he said, his eyes a blazing jet. 'Oh, yes. Wait for me. Hold on. I'll be there.'

Without a backward glance, he strode hastily from the room.

She ate a little supper when it arrived. However distraught she was, Hassan's lovemaking had sapped her strength and Tiffany must have slept, for when she woke she was still lying on the bed, totally naked, and Hassan lay beside her, caressing her body, the darkness of his skin contrasting with hers. He smiled.

'Please don't touch me,' she whispered.

'Sleepy?' He gave an indulgent laugh and curled her body into his. Immediately she felt safe in his strong arms. Safe! How wrong could her instincts be?

'Relax,' he crooned. 'You're as tense as a high wire. I'm perfectly capable of sleeping with you and not making love. There's more to a relationship than that.'

'Trust,' she quavered.

'Ah. Yes.' His mouth murmured against her temple. 'I can wait for that. It's a small word but has a huge meaning. I can't deny that I'm unsure of your motives. Still, you were young when you married Nazim and became pregnant. I can understand how you resented being tied down.'

She blinked, upset at his arrogance. She'd meant that she didn't trust *him*!

She lay very still for a long time before she spoke, knowing how important this was. Her first chance to clear her character in his eyes.

'You want the truth, you'll get it,' she said bitterly. 'I'll tell you about Nazim. I met him when I was eighteen. I was emotionally young. When you train for the ballet, you have no time for boyfriends. I was pitifully ripe for his attentions and his domination. We met at a dance, in the School of Oriental and African Studies where I was doing a course in oriental design. He came as a guest of one of the tutors. I let him drive me home and he stopped the car in a dark spot to kiss me.'

'That's enough. I don't want to hear what you did with him.'

Hassan had rolled over. She stared miserably at his back.

'You have to,' she cried. 'God! I don't want to talk about this! But you must know the kind of man your brother was and the kind of woman I am!'

'Tiffany,' he said urgently, turning to face her again, pain etched in the lines of his hard mouth. 'I refuse to listen to your account of his courtship.'

'Courtship?' She let out a rasping laugh. 'Nazim only knew about having sex,' she said tightly. 'Not love. Not romance, or courting.'

Hassan's eyes narrowed. 'What do you mean? I thought—Tiffany! Tell me!' he demanded roughly.

'He seemed to imagine that, because I'd let him kiss me, he could go on from there as far as he wanted, as if I'd given him unlimited permission. I didn't know that by giving in to his pleas to touch me I was storing up trouble for myself,' she said bitterly. 'I couldn't stop him,

Hassan. He was like a maniac...' She gulped and Hassan enfolded her in his arms, soothing her shaking body.

'He all but raped me,' she said harshly. 'I called out but no one came. It was late in the evening and no one was around. He took what he wanted. He said I'd driven him to it, that I'd enticed him with my body—the way I'd danced with him, swaying, with my hair falling over my eyes, the way I walked past him, the way I provocatively lifted my breasts when speaking passionately about something...I didn't know! I swear I didn't!'

He stared into her eyes, and she wished she knew what he was seeing there. Could he recognise her anguish?

'Did he touch you again?' he asked grimly.

'No. I made sure of that. But he kept pestering me, day in, day out. And then I discovered I was pregnant.'

'And?'

'I told my mother and she found his address and went straight to him, saying he had to marry me or he'd be in trouble. It wasn't my idea——'

'But you married him,' growled Hassan.

'I didn't want to! At first he was angry. He came to my home and we had a blazing row. That's when he struck me and I fell down the stairs. But the fact that I nearly lost my baby changed Nazim—and me. We were both appalled. He felt terribly responsible and did, at least, care about our baby. He visited me in hospital and... well, we both really wanted our child. He seemed so devoted, so sorry—I thought he loved me.' She bit her lip, speaking in an almost incoherent babble, desperate to convince him. 'I had to believe in his love. Mother made it clear that I was guilty of immorality and lack of control. I could hardly forgive myself. There were flowers and chocolates, and he was gentle, Hassan, kind and thoughtful. And I wanted the best for my child. He said love would grow, that we'd make a fresh start.

was young, with no qualifications and a repressive mother. I couldn't bear the idea of bringing up a child under those conditions. Nazim was very persuasive in the picture he painted.'

Hassan gently stroked her hair, his eyes dark.

'Nazim was always persuasive. I must remind you, though, that he said in his letter that you hated being pregnant.'

'I hated being constantly sick. I hated living in a one-room bedsit. I hated the discovery that I'd made a terrible mistake about Nazim. Because once we were married, he didn't have to bother to be nice to me and we quarrelled incessantly. He wanted my body and didn't care if I felt like making love or not. Sometimes he was so rough that I was afraid for the child within me. You must believe me, Hassan; I continued with my studies because I could see that one day I'd need to support myself and my child—and maybe Nazim too. We were already in debt from his extravagance.'

A frown crossed his face. 'I can't recall that flaw in his character as a young man,' he said in an accusing tone.

'You don't believe me,' she moaned, twisting away.

He brought her back to him, holding her so that she was forced to look into his relentless, questioning eyes.

'You have to tell me your side of it,' he said, his face cold.

'Hassan,' she said in an impassioned voice, 'Nazim had everything he wanted, living with you and your father. Money could buy everything. Maybe when he left and had to manage on his own, he found it hard because he'd never been taught to budget. He really had no idea about keeping accounts and paying bills promptly. We lived well above our means because he'd deny himself nothing. What he wanted, he had. Including me,' she said bitterly.

'Let's get some sleep,' muttered Hassan. 'I find it painful in the extreme to think of my brother making love to you.'

'He never did,' she said in a small voice. 'Not love. He never did.'

For a moment, Tiffany thought he was going to take her in his arms. But then darkness shuttered his face and killed all expression.

'I have possessed your body,' he said quietly. 'I'm not sure I'll ever possess more. My relationship with Nazim is too close, isn't it?'

'I can't be sure if you're like him,' she whispered, her eyes rounded in distress.

He shrugged. 'Then you must find out. It will be enough to begin with—to have you as a wife, for us to know that Josef has a bright future, and that we can find pleasure in bed together. More may come, but we can't expect it, Tiffany.'

'Why am I destined to make loveless marriages?' she cried.

'Go to sleep,' he muttered.

She lay for hours, staring miserably at the great breadth of his back, the golden skin shining in the moonlight which filtered through the carved shutters. Her eyes travelled down his spine and across the wide shoulders. He lay very still, hardly breathing.

Her brilliant plan to allay his suspicions had probably worked. But at a terrible cost to herself. She'd virtually offered herself as a sacrifice. How it had happened, she didn't know, but whenever he came near all sense disappeared, to be replaced by a helpless surrender, as if destiny was telling her that this was the man she must devote herself to whether it destroyed her or not.

In the early morning, while it was still dark, they woke and made love, exploring, plundering, savouring each other's bodies. And it was tearing her apart, inch by inch, breaking her as he had sworn he would if she played false.

Later, as dawn tinged the room with blushing gold, she stroked his rosy-hued face, her mind drifting in all directions. It was as if they were already married and Jo was next door, and at breakfast he and Hassan would fill the house with laughter.

'Thinking of last night?' Hassan murmured, his hand reaching out to stroke her thigh.

She blushed, reminded of her abandon. He chuckled and leapt out of bed, striding to the shower.

When he whirled around and caught her admiring his perfect body, he grinned. Tiffany lowered her lashes.

'I was thinking of Jo,' she said quietly. 'How you made him laugh on the phone yesterday...' Her voice trailed away, wistful. He was wonderful with Jo.

'You miss him very much, don't you?' he said, coming over and taking her in his arms.

She looked up at him, pleading that he'd believe her.

'Yes, I do! Terribly! I want...' There was a catch in her voice. 'I want to be with him again.'

'It won't be long. A couple of days.'

He tucked her head into his smooth shoulder and rocked her gently, stroking her hair. Tiffany felt a wonderful feeling of peace. It filled her with anguish to think that she might soon be running away from Hassan. Very soon; it had to be. Or could she stay? Her head ached with her see-sawing decisions. She'd never been indecisive before. Hassan had reduced her to this. He'd taken away all her strength.

'Be patient,' he continued, murmuring in her ear. 'Life waits for us as a family together. Standing on touch-lines, yelling ourselves hoarse, skiing in Switzerland or Morocco, lazing on a yacht off the coast of Zanzibar, coping with Josef's taste in music when he has birthday parties——'

'You make it sound wonderful,' she said shakily, wishing that the world he described could belong to her. Inside, a small voice was telling her that it could, torturing her remorselessly.

'It will be. We've grown above our misunderstandings and hate, Tiffany. You've seen a little of the way I am, day by day. I couldn't pay my staff to behave towards me as they do. I must have some redeeming features for them to be at ease with me, mustn't I?' He smiled.

'I can't understand why you want to take on Josef and me.'

His hands cupped the sides of her face and he gazed at her long and tenderly.

'Losing my brother was hard enough,' he said. 'My father never fully recovered from the shock. But at least I can make everything straight again, and ensure Josef carries on the Sharif name. And you know why I want to "take you on" as you so romantically put it,' he teased.

'Why did Nazim leave?' she asked.

That was the key to all of this. Instinctively she knew that it would explain something of her late husband's character and behaviour, and throw light on Hassan himself.

His lashes dropped to hide the wary light in his eyes.

'I can't answer that. I dislike having secrets from you, but someone else will have to tell you the reason, not me. And somehow I doubt that you'll ever know. I can't risk causing distress to another person who is an essential part of my life.'

'Faridah.' She looked at him hopelessly, torn with jealousy.

Seeing that she trembled uncontrollably, he abruptly removed his hands from her face and moved to the shower.

'Faridah does mean something to you, doesn't she?' cried Tiffany piteously. 'Oh, God! How can I bear this?'

'Faridah is my cousin and under my protection because I'm the oldest living male relative,' he said stiffly. 'I can't discuss her business.'

'Not even with me? Not even if it's partly *your* business?' she cried angrily.

His head went up. 'I'm going down to breakfast in a few minutes. Join me there if you want to.'

Tiffany couldn't. She stayed immobile while Hassan showered, dressed and went out.

Her mind kept vacillating, tormenting her with memories of Hassan's lovemaking and persuading her that they could have a marvellous life, the three of them.

Abdul had the first claim on the Sharif name and fortune—far more than she or Josef. In fact, she didn't care if she had nothing other than Hassan himself and Jo.

Confused, she slipped down to the garden, hoping to find some mental space to think. But she found Hassan sitting gloomily on a seat, his head in his hands. Her heart went out to him. He looked so miserable, so haunted, and when he saw her compassionate face his expression of joy burned so deep into her soul that she knew she had already fallen in love with him and everything was too late to be stopped.

She was his, body and soul, heart and mind.

His past was not important. Only their future.

He held out his arms in a pleading gesture and she gave a low moan and ran into them. For a long time they didn't move, but held each other tightly as if afraid a small part would escape and not be included in the fervent expression of love and need.

'I want to tell you, sweetheart,' he whispered to her. 'But I can't. I'll speak to Faridah. I'll tell her it's coming between us.'

'No. I think she's been hurt enough,' said Tiffany, her eyes shining with unshed tears. 'And, in any case, I think I needed that time to myself. I came to a decision.'

Slowly he drew back, his face anxious. 'Go on.'

She was about to tell him that she loved him, to pour out all her feelings and put herself completely at his mercy. But the sound of Faridah's voice cut through the still air like a knife and thrust into her heart.

'Tell me,' urged Hassan.

'Not now——'

'Damn! Over here, Faridah!' he yelled in an angry tone. 'What the hell is it?'

'A phone call. Urgent. From Marcia,' she said coldly, eyeing Tiffany up and down.

'I must go. I've been expecting this. It could take some time. Meet you at noon to chat to Josef.' Hassan gave her a quick kiss on the lips, and followed it with a helpless, more lingering one.

Tiffany clutched at him, not wanting him to go. Faridah gloomily watched him stride away and then sat down beside her.

'He has us all in the palm of his hand,' she muttered. 'He runs our lives and we hardly know he's doing so.'

'I'm sorry if my presence——'

'You'll be sorry, if you don't get away,' Faridah burst out.

A nameless fear raised the hairs on the back of Tiffany's neck. 'Are you threatening me?' she asked, her eyes worried.

'I? Threaten? My God! You've got more to worry about than a mere jealous woman! Oh, yes, I'm jealous. I don't deny that. I love Hassan. I've known him for years and you walk into his life and into his bed in a matter of moments.'

'Oh, Faridah! It isn't quite like that——'

'Your morals aren't my concern. Hassan is a healthy man and took what was on offer.'

'No——'

'You think there's any other reason? I pity you!' scathed Faridah. 'More, I pity your son and the danger you place him in.'

'What?' she cried, alerted by the woman's genuine fear.

'Oh, for goodness' sake!' cried Faridah impatiently. 'Pull yourself together! Hassan has softened your brain. I suppose he pretended he was going to marry you?'

'Pretended? He...what do you mean? Why do you say that?' demanded Tiffany.

'He's spoken for. I told you that, but you wouldn't listen. It's a long-standing arrangement,' said Faridah.

'But he said——'

Tiffany stopped, aghast. How could he have denied the existence of the arrangement? Faridah must be lying.

'He's not likely to admit it, if he wants to get you into bed, is he?' scathed Faridah. 'He won't touch me, of course, till our wedding day. Think; you've got a brain. Is he likely to marry his brother's wife, a used woman? He'll visualise Nazim's hands on you every time he looks at you. Besides, you're English and have a questionable reputation. He used you to sate his hunger because he couldn't approach me. I'm not that kind of woman. You're different. He's making the most of you, while you're around and so easily available.'

'Using me?' she repeated faintly.

'Of course. You've underestimated him. A disastrous mistake where you're concerned. He's been enjoying your sexual favours and blinding you to his real intentions.'

'Are you suggesting that he's been deliberately allaying my suspicions?' Tiffany laughed incredulously. That had been *her* plan! It was too ludicrous for words!

'He succeeded, didn't he? All your anger, all the fight has gone out of you. You're putty in his hands. He can do anything he likes with you now. Soon you will innocently invite Josef here, and that'll be the end of him.'

She went cold, unable to move, searching Faridah's face. It was remorseless.

'The end?' she whispered, suddenly petrified.

Faridah's face twisted savagely, making her look ugly. 'There will be an accident,' she grated. 'I know it. How else will he make sure your son doesn't live to make any claims on the business?'

Tiffany began to shake. 'Doesn't live? An accident? But—Faridah, you can't mean ... no, no,' she moaned.

Faridah was talking about the man who'd made passionate love to her, who'd shared the days in friendship, looked at her with loving eyes. Lying eyes. Lying hands, mouth, fingers ...

'See sense,' said Faridah. 'He wants you out of the way. And your son. He has other plans.'

Tiffany's head jerked up. 'Oh, my God!' she whispered. 'Abdul!' she cried wildly.

'What?' snapped Faridah, her eyes narrowed.

'Abdul! I know of his existence, you can't deny it! Abdul al Sharif. He's Hassan's illegitimate son, isn't he? Are you his mother? You must tell me!'

Faridah looked taken aback. Slowly she nodded.

'Abdul. Yes. How did you find out?'

'I heard Hassan talking on the phone about your son,' croaked Tiffany. 'He's planning to switch some of his US holdings to Abdul. And I suppose Josef is a problem because he stands in Abdul's way.'

A slow smile spread over Faridah's face. 'How generous he is! Oh, yes,' she nodded. 'How clever of you to find out. Yes. Abdul is the reason for all this. Hassan directs all his passion towards getting what he wants, as you know.' She ran her eyes insultingly over Tiffany's body.

'He wouldn't stoop to hurt Jo! It isn't true, say it isn't true,' cried Tiffany desperately.

'As you please,' shrugged Faridah, standing up to go. 'Be it on your own head. Does it sound likely that he intends to marry you and let your son inherit, when Abdul can do so? If you don't come to your senses, it'll be too late. You'll have a dead child on your hands.'

'*Dead!* Oh, my God! Wait!' Tiffany's legs shook so much from terror that she couldn't stand, but was reduced to sitting helplessly and pleading with Faridah with her eyes. 'Help me,' she begged. 'Help me to escape from this terrible nightmare! Help me to leave this place and find some sanity!'

Triumph flared in Faridah's face. 'You want to leave?'

'Yes! Now!' cried Tiffany wildly. 'I must get back to Josef at once; I don't ever want to see Hassan again, to hear his voice, to feel...' Her voice broke and it was several seconds before she could continue in a desolate, bleak tone. 'I must get away before Hassan shames me any more. I have to prevent him from holding me here as a hostage and blackmailing me to get Josef over to Riyam. Please, Faridah! It's in your own interest to help me!'

'It is. I need you out of the way too,' she acknowledged sharply. 'Tonight. Meet me in the garden after midnight. I'll show you where to find a camel,' she offered. 'I'll bring food and water for you. All I can do is point you in the right direction. I daren't do more. I'm afraid of his anger. Well?'

'Please,' mumbled Tiffany, swaying with the enormity of what she was about to do. 'How safe is it, in the desert?' she asked, in a dry, ragged voice. 'How will I know where to go?'

'Stick to the trail,' said Faridah. 'He'll be tied up tomorrow, with his legal officer who's flown in from America. If you can keep him out of your bed tonight and escape, then it'll be ages before he notices you're gone. And then you'll be safe.'

'Why not now?' urged Tiffany, her eyes huge. She couldn't face a whole day and then evening here with her son's potential murderer. And if she had time to think of the terror of the desert journey, she might never make it.

'Because if you didn't come down to dinner, he'd notice you were missing, you fool,' said Faridah scornfully.

'Oh, yes. Of course.' Tiffany's brain seemed to be filled with a dense fog. 'Faridah, I can't spend the evening with him.'

'You have to,' she said in a hard tone. 'He must never suspect. Don't you think he'll be wary if you avoid him? Don't you realise he'll come up to see you, and maybe take advantage of you again if you're lying on the bed pretending to be ill?'

Tiffany let out a sigh of utter despair. 'I can't pretend——'

'For the sake of your child, you will. You must let him think nothing's wrong,' snapped Faridah.

In fact, Tiffany was able to spend the day alone. Hassan had sent someone to meet Marcia who had arrived at Shirbat airport and they both stayed in his office, working on papers and taking lunch there.

Shortly before dinner, with Tiffany once again steeling herself to get dressed and face Hassan with a bright mask, Faridah came to her room, carrying a tray.

'I thought you might need a drink,' she said.

'Damn right I do,' muttered Tiffany, taking a good gulp. Faridah laughed at her expression when the alcohol hit her throat. 'What is that?' croaked Tiffany, feeling as if she'd swallowed neat turpentine.

'Local brew. It's OK. It'll give you courage.'

'It'll give me a sore throat.'

'Drink,' insisted Faridah. 'It'll relax you. Tonight you've got to make sure Hassan really believes he's landed you in his net. And then you've got to stop him sleeping with you. Can you manage that?'

Tiffany took another cautious drink and felt her stomach warm and her courage grow stronger. Faridah was eyeing the neat blue suit on the bed with distaste and strode over to Tiffany's wardrobe, pushing back hanger after hanger as she assessed the clothes inside.

'Be a sexy ice-maiden. You've got the face for it.'

She threw the strapless black sheath on to the bed.

'There's a jacket I wear with that——' began Tiffany. She sat down. The drink was paralysing her legs.

'Wear it without. Don't you see? If you look seductive and yet rebuff his advances, he'll realise you're not going to be easily dominated.'

Tiffany passed a hand over her head. She didn't understand the logic. Her brain buzzed.

'Wouldn't it be better if I wore something demure?' she puzzled.

'Do as I say. You're in no fit state to think straight. This is a much more subtle method. He won't suspect anything this way. Get it on. If necessary, I'll keep him from slipping up to your room, but it'll be better if you can cool him down yourself.'

Faridah stayed to help the dazed Tiffany get ready and made sure she went down the stairs to the salon. Tiffany didn't know what she was doing, only that she felt numb with cold and terror. Soon she'd be travelling across a hostile desert. She was mad. But desperate.

Hassan, in a dinner-jacket, was talking to a curly-haired blonde woman wearing an elegant green silk suit. Suddenly Tiffany felt cheap in her dress, and gazed down on the considerable swell of her breasts and deep cleavage in dismay. What was she doing? Why had she listened to Faridah? The woman's motives couldn't be entirely innocent.

It was too late. Hassan had turned at the woman's surprise at the sight of Tiffany and his startled look was overlaid with a predatory hunger which made Tiffany melt within as if her bones flowed.

He made the introductions and she was aware of his eyes on her, piercing into her muddled brain.

'Marcia, would you excuse us for a moment? Tiffany and I have a quick arrangement to make,' he said smoothly. 'Please make yourself comfortable in the salon. I'll be in shortly.'

'Sure,' smiled Marcia. 'I'll wait for you there.'

At Hassan's steady, serious gaze, Tiffany swayed a little and clutched at a curtain for support. Then she felt his iron grip on her arm and she was being hustled into an ante-room, her body strangely unresponsive and heavy. She stumbled and he drew her up roughly.

His curse made her flinch and widen her eyes.

'Say something,' he rasped, his face close to hers.

'What? Hassan——'

'I thought so!' He frowned. 'You've been drinking! What the hell has happened? And for God's sake, what on earth made you appear half-naked tonight?'

She tried to shrink away from him, but he pulled her to his body ruthlessly.

'Am I now beginning to see the real Tiffany Sharif?' he asked. 'Are you truly a loose, sex-loving, promiscuous woman? After all, you haven't yet explained away Mike to my satisfaction.'

'Mike?' She tried to remember who he was, her mouth pouting in effort.

The grip on her arm tightened. 'So many men you can't remember? You've got me so I don't know what I'm doing! I hardly know what to believe about you, only that you throw out a carnal challenge to me which I can't resist.'

His head bent to her high rising breasts, his hands pulling down her precarious top, and she threw back her head and let out a groan. It was unbearable to have him hating her like this, but it helped her to keep control of herself.

What had Faridah said? Stop him sleeping with you tonight. Inspiration leapt into her mind.

'Don't touch me,' she said in a voice of loathing. 'I've tried to forget him, but I can't. Every time you made love to me, he was in my thoughts. It was he whom I held in my arms, who kissed me, not you.'

Hassan had let her go, and she felt his heavy breath rasping through his bared teeth.

'He?' he whispered hoarsely.

She fixed slightly glazed eyes on him. 'Why do you think I got a little tipsy tonight? I can't carry on unless I obliterate my conscious mind. He. Nazim.'

'You said that you hated him, that he raped you——'

'How else could I get your sympathy?' she asked recklessly.

There was a deathly silence. Tiffany couldn't bear to look at his ashen face, drained of life.

'I've got a headache,' she muttered. 'I'll give dinner a miss.'

'Wait.'

Racked by the anguish in his voice, she tried to understand why it should be there. This was the man who wanted to harm Josef. Yet it seemed he had really felt affection for her. Had Faridah been wrong? If only her brain wasn't so fuzzy!

'Go up to your room and stay there,' he said coldly.

'You won't come——'

'No,' he whispered. 'I never want to touch you again. You've caused me too much heartache, Tiffany. You were right. I will never be sure if you're faking or not. You cold bitch!' His hand thudded down hard on a table, making everything on it jump, and she cowered back a little.

'I suppose you want me to leave in the morning,' she said as casually as possible. Hope and despair battled within her. She might not have to go the hard way. He might send her packing himself. How could she want that and feel so miserable at the same time?

'Leave?' he snarled. 'When I don't have Josef? Oh, no. The situation is as it stood when you first arrived. I want my nephew and I'll go to any lengths now to get him. You stay here. The difference is that I won't marry you. Instead, I'll take my revenge on you for the way you've treated me by attacking you where it will hurt most.'

She met his glittering eyes with a terror-stricken look.

'Not Jo!'

He smiled a slow, cynical smile.

'I won't be beaten by a conniving, deceiving whore,' he said softly.

Swaying, she struggled for strength. Damn Faridah and her whisky! With a few shreds of dignity, she tipped up her head and carefully put one foot in front of the other, till she had left the room. The die had been cast. She would escape from this living hell.

Upstairs, she stripped off the black sheath and crawled into bed, shaking, waiting. The hours dragged. Near midnight, she dressed with fumbling, trembling fingers, putting on the green tunic and trousers and picking up the chador.

The garden rustled with sounds of the night and a light, whispering breeze. She sat on a bench and waited. A small lizard ran splay-footed near her listless hand. This beautiful garden, this lovely house, would be denied Josef. And Hassan—the only man, she knew, who could ever rouse her to such heights of passion—was to be denied her. A sob broke from her lips.

She wanted him; she had loved him. She wanted to repeat that wonderful moment when passion had been spent and they lay in each other's arms, cradled tenderly, as if they loved one another.

'Come.'

She jumped at Faridah's sharp voice. Casually they strolled past servants as if going for a night-time stroll, and through the main gates to the camel park. Faridah gave some money to the man and they helped Tiffany on, packing food and water into the panniers.

'It's only a few hours,' said Faridah. 'Go! Hurry!'

She slapped the animal on the rump. It lurched up and Tiffany made herself secure in the saddle, her heart in her mouth. She pulled on the reins, following the direction of the man's pointing finger, along a well-marked trail into the night.

After a little while she felt confident that she could handle the swaying movement and urged the animal into a shambling trot.

She had no idea how long it would be before Hassan discovered she was missing. She'd have to get out of Riyam fast and lie low for some time. For one thing was certain—all hell would be let loose.

Uncomfortably, she joggled on the camel's back, every rangy, loping stride taking her nearer to Josef and further from the rapacious Hassan.

Dawn filtered the sky with rose, red and purple. Soon the hard light of day beat down and she slowed the camel to a walk as the warm sun warmed her bones.

But almost immediately, the camel started snorting and bellowing, tossing its head alarmingly, and it was all she could do to keep her balance. A sixth sense made her turn around.

The sky was an unusual colour. A band of bright yellow stained the horizon, far to the north, on her left. It wasn't the dawn. She frowned, wondering.

Small spirals of sand twirled and coiled in the distance, like miniature whirlwinds. An uncanny sensation crept down her spine. The minute tornados were too tiny to harm her, but the air seemed to be tense, as if holding its breath, and she felt oddly nervous and jittery.

Thunder rolled in the south, where the sky glowered with dark navy thunderclouds. Tiffany eyed them anxiously and drove the jumpy camel onwards at a furious pace, clinging to the saddle for dear life.

The light grew dim and the air thickened, increasing in density and temperature until she was fighting for breath in a wall of suffocating heat. The sky had become an eerie yellow ahead, but she thought she had to continue, to avoid the thunderstorm. She looked up as a chill settled over her and discovered that the sun had disappeared. It had been obliterated by the yellow sky.

A bitter cold and damp wind swept over her, freezing every inch of her body. And it was then that she realised what was happening.

Her stomach lurched. Nausea clawed in her throat.

A brown wall of dust was coming towards her, closing with a petrifying speed. Amid the vast emptiness, she felt frighteningly alone, nothing more than a tiny, lone figure, a minute speck in the vast desert, easily swept away by any capricious force of nature. The cloud rolled inexorably on, and now she heard a mind-numbing wailing and grinding—the noise of sand being picked up and forced into the billowing blanket.

It was a sandstorm, and it was coming straight for her.

The years of self-discipline as a dancer, and of fighting for survival when Nazim had left her, came to her rescue. Her natural reaction was to fight trouble, especially as Josef was far away, depending on her.

People didn't die in sandstorms. They became lost if they went off course. She must keep her head, and when it became too difficult to carry on she must dismount and hang on to the camel's reins so they weren't parted. It was her lifeline.

Her terrified eyes never left the great column of swirling sand. It grew every second, whisking up small stunted trees and bushes in its path, and she could see them being hurled into the air. Panic rose within her.

Josef. Her beloved son. She had to come out of this for his sake! *Hassan!* Oh, dear God, she'd loved him! She'd needed him to live, as a dying man needed water. Without him, she would be only half a woman.

Her emotions were one turbulent storm, wrenching her apart by the violence of intense feelings which would never be calmed, but would blind her cruelly to any other man's affection, wearing down her spirit like rasping sand until she was left raw and wounded. Hassan was destroying her. And here, in this terrible desert, the sandstorm was finishing the job.

The camel balked beneath her, tossing its head, bellowing in rage. It wanted to go in the opposite direction and Tiffany had to force it to stay on the right path. Gently she urged it to kneel, intending to shelter and trusting in its instincts. It was built to withstand conditions like this. Didn't it have extra eyelids? Or was it some kind of special nostril? she thought wildly.

The animal wouldn't kneel. Frantically, weeping with frustration, yelling out loud, she pulled on the reins.

And then, over the roar of the fast-approaching cloud, she heard the unbelievable, wonderful sound of an engine.

Turning, the wind tearing away the shawl over her head so that her hair was whipped into stinging lashes over her face, she saw a green truck driving hell for leather towards her. She held up the shawl and let it stream in the wind like a banner. The camel folded its legs under and she slipped out of the saddle, still clutching the reins and her banner.

Then her hand faltered. The truck was by now close enough for her to recognise the dark head which was thrust out of the window. Only one man could have that same broad face and sweep of forehead, the terrible, glittering fury.

Hassan was driving fast, and with such hatred on his face that she drew back against the camel's flank.

The material slipped from her frozen fingers and disappeared in a trice with the icy wind. The truck stalled and he cursed loudly. He was angry. Violently angry. And Faridah had warned her of his vengeance.

The truck started again. Her hair was half-blinding her as she fumbled for the saddle, hoping to mount, running like a frightened rabbit from the man who was almost upon her, and shouting at the top of his voice. He was merciless and single-minded. He would stop at nothing.

CHAPTER EIGHT

TERROR blocking her mind, Tiffany fumbled with the reins, trying to mount in the teeth of the fierce eddies which brought stinging sand to blast into her face and the corners of her mouth. She shut her eyes tightly.

A strong gust buffeted her and she fell, only to scream with panic at the hard jolt of Hassan's body against hers. Grains of grit lashed into her mouth, half choking her. She struggled, but her endurance had been tested to the limit and she could fight no more.

Hassan dragged her roughly over the ground and pushed her into the truck in a bundle of limp arms and legs. The door slammed. The merciless sandpaper gale ceased and she felt soft leather against her back and thighs and a blessed warmth.

'You fool! You stupid fool!' roared Hassan.

She turned her face away, but he caught her head and made her look at him. She blinked to free her lashes from sand and gagged on the grit in her mouth. He reached behind him and drew a soft cloth over her face, delicately sweeping sand from her hair, brows and lashes, grimly tipping her head back and tousling her hair so that no more grains would fall on her face.

'Why?' he barked, his finger and thumb gripping her chin so hard that she cried out.

'Because I know what you feel about me!' she cried hysterically.

The truck rocked alarmingly, battered by a blast of wind. An involuntary scream escaped from Tiffany's lips and Hassan half crushed her in his arms.

'Don't touch me!' she said, cringing.

The wind-borne sand screeched across the dark green paintwork of the truck like an electrical sander. Hassan ignored her attempts to avoid him and drew her down beneath him.

Her body was plastered against his as violent gusts lashed the windscreen, scraping it with a terrifying sound. She spoke, but didn't hear her own voice. The wind was roaring louder than she could yell.

Protest was useless. They were trapped there together and when the storm ended he would make sure she returned. Or he might leave her there to die. Her brain cleared for a moment. Why hadn't he done that? Why not leave her outside?

A rush of pebbles fell on the roof and bonnet, for all the world as if they were knocking to come in. The noise of the shower deafened her. She let her arms creep around Hassan's neck and his embrace tightened. Shifting his position, he moved so that his entire body protected hers and he was lying across her. His cheek lay against hers, their mouths a mere movement of the head away. Tiffany's lashes fluttered, signalling her agitation.

Hassan's eyes slanted over to hers.

The pounding of her heart sounded as loud to her as the roar outside. Something heavy careened into the car, making it shudder and bounce on its springs. She screamed soundlessly, her vocal cords paralysed with fear.

Hassan was saying something. She frowned. Then her mouth was covered with warmth—soft, seeping warmth, which calmed her and made her think of other things instead of the danger they were in.

His lips moved away, to leave her bereft. But she felt the racing of his heart against her breast and her pulses quickened in exultation.

Madness! A wild elation was surging through her body; the storm outside and within were somehow merging, making her want to fire off all her energy. And then she realised. He hadn't wanted to kill her, or he would have left her to suffer the sandstorm alone. He wanted her badly enough to drive hell for leather over the desert and save her.

She couldn't quite make it out. The noise outside was too great for her to think clearly. All she knew was that Hassan held her with a fierce, protective tenderness, and although she couldn't hear it she could feel his breath as his voice soothed her.

There was an explanation. She would find it.

The hammering of the pebble storm abated. In its place, accompanied by a sudden rushing sound as if a waterfall hit them, came torrents of thick mud, driving at them in a horizontal brown mass. It drove so hard into the truck that it shuddered with the force and mud splattered through a dozen hairline gaps, covering her face, her hands and arms, all that was exposed. She could feel it clinging to Hassan's body, plastering him in brown sludge in seconds.

A howling wind arose, deafening her, ringing in her ears and through her head till she felt her brain must explode. Nothing, surely, could withstand this relentless beating—neither the truck, nor its occupants. They were certain to die. Any moment now, one of the gusts which perilously rocked the truck would turn it over and batter the vehicle until their bodies were exposed to the merciless storm.

'Hassan!' she yelled. 'I love you!'

She heard nothing. Neither had he. A profound sense of misery engulfed her. She was to die, never to see her son again, clasped in the arms of the man she loved, without settling the misunderstandings between them. To die with a lie on her conscience.

The mockery of the situation lanced through her in a sharp pain. She wouldn't be here if it weren't for Hassan. In discovering—too late—what was really important in her life, she was to be denied the chance to fight for it.

Driving rain sheeted down in a continuous wall of grey lead. Something massive smashed into the windscreen with such a force that they both grabbed each other in shock, gasping at the icy deluge which drenched them in seconds. Hassan desperately tried to cover her completely.

Flicking a narrowed eye at the windscreen, Tiffany saw that a tree had been driven against the truck, buckling the reinforced steel surround of the windscreen and shattering the glass. There was another impact and Hassan's body shuddered and became inert over her.

Her face muffled against his shoulder, she tried to move him, to no avail. The tumult rose to a crescendo. Another onslaught of grit and sand blasted the truck, sweeping it in a violent turbulence which threw them about inside.

Painfully bruised, Tiffany tried to protect Hassan, but he slowly, painfully, reached for her and covered her with his body again, a look of anguish on his face. A feeling of intense relief washed through her, making her whole body weak with joy and relief.

He was alive. She began to sob.

Flesh to flesh, bone to bone, they seemed united against the elements. Two bodies moulded into one, two hearts beating in unison, their lips touching and tasting each laboured breath, sharing a life experience that was theirs alone and bound them to one another more surely than anything else.

Her mouth moved on his and was immediately possessed in a smouldering kiss so fierce that she forgot everything around her—all sound, all fear, all danger. The kiss went on and on, her lips imprinted and branded by a glorious never-ending passion which reached way inside her mind.

'Oh, Tiffany,' he groaned.

She blinked. She'd heard! Hassan lifted himself back a little, the shock showing in his startled eyes.

'It's over,' he said hoarsely. There was a note of despair in his voice. 'It's over,' came the whispered words from his unhappy mouth.

Warily, he twisted around, scowling at his surroundings. Then he pushed himself right up on his arms to the seat beside her and wrenched at the door-handle.

'Be careful!' she cried, unable to stop herself.

He paused, as if she'd hit him, then swung his legs to the ground. After a moment, she followed, stiff and aching. It was an extraordinary scene. A pile of storm-blown debris lay heaped against the truck. The whole vehicle had been laid bare, stripped to naked metal.

'The truck is ruined!' she gasped.

'But we are alive.'

She turned slowly to look at him and he tipped his head back to massage his neck, then fixed her with an intense stare which made the breath catch in her throat.

His face was streaked with caked mud and red dust and she loved him more than she could ever say in words. When his expression became a grimace, she suddenly stared down at her own body. It was filthy. Her hand reached up and touched tangled, caked rats' tails which had once been her golden hair.

The wind dropped. The storm passed and it was as if a veil had lifted. She saw everything with enormous clarity. Everything.

She loved Hassan with a passion that surmounted all barriers.

'We need some water,' he muttered. 'There's some in the truck.'

He poured her a flask and it tasted like champagne. Her eyes sparkled appreciatively, but he didn't return her smiling look. He had tightened his mouth in disapproval.

'You might have been killed,' he rasped. 'Why? For God's sake, why risk your stupid neck by taking a camel into the desert? Am I that repugnant to you? Why the hell didn't you say so in the first place, instead of pretending and giving me the wrong impression?'

It hurt his pride, she thought sadly. He hated being fooled.

'I wanted to escape,' she said, a wistful look in her eyes. Now the storm was over, she found it hard to tell him what she felt. 'I didn't know there would be a sandstorm.'

'You must loathe and fear me very deeply. Come. I'll take you to clean up. Then you can make arrangements to fly to Oman.'

'To Josef?' she cried.

He turned his back on her. 'To Josef.'

There was misery in his body, in every agonised muscle.

'You're giving in?' she asked quietly. 'You've given up what you sought so single-mindedly?'

'I know when I'm beaten,' he grated. 'Follow me.'

She hesitated, then hurried after his dejected figure. Sand and mud had made their way into every part of her, it seemed. She caught up with him.

The ragged-edged sun's strength was weak. It must be late, but somehow the day seemed timeless. And the desert was blooming. Before her eyes, daisies and huge buttercups were spreading bright carpets across sand where once there had been only barren ground. Butterflies appeared from nowhere to take delight in the nodding blooms.

Hassan was taking no pleasure from them. He stopped near a circular whitewashed wall, and when Tiffany drew nearer she could see that a flight of steps led downwards into the ground. He descended and turned to make sure she followed.

'It's a ventilation shaft,' he said tonelessly. 'Only twenty feet down. Can you make it?'

'I'm afraid of nothing after that storm.' She smiled, reaching out her hand.

He ignored it and went on down. Once inside, she found it cool on her hot, caked skin. The steps wound down and finally arrived at a stone platform lit by warm gold light from above. Ahead lay a midnight-black pool, and to one side a pipe emptied into the pool like a miniature waterfall.

'What is this place?' she asked in wonder.

'A *felaj*. An underground aqueduct. Built by the Persians, two thousand years ago.'

'Where does the water come from?'

'Mountain springs. It's cold, but the sun will have warmed it a little.'

He mechanically slipped off his boots and tunic till he wore only his thin cotton trousers, and dived in as if she didn't exist.

She was annoyed. He spent all his energies in making her lust after him and then switched off! But he'd relented. He was letting her go back to Jo and ending his cruel attempt to dominate her. She could be strong now.

Unless ... She caught Hassan's dark, scowling eyes on her and drew back, suddenly afraid.

'Oh, for heaven's sake, Tiffany,' he raged at her, all control gone. 'I'm not going to drown you! Why the hell would I kill someone I love?'

She froze. 'That's cruel,' she whispered.

'Cruel?' he muttered, gripping the side of the pool and staring up at her with a haunted expression. 'That's rich! You make me mindless with desire, you drive me insane with jealousy, you repeatedly thrust knives into me by taunting me about your relationship with Nazim, and you say I'm cruel?'

She crouched down, beginning to see what he was saying, her eyes rapidly scanning his face for proof.

'I didn't like being treated like a sex object——'

'You were never that,' he said huskily. 'You were a celebration. It was like worship for me, touching you, knowing what we could do to each other.'

'Hassan!' she said slowly, in astonishment. He was serious. Deadly serious. 'I didn't mean what I said about Nazim. I regret my lie now. But I said it to stop you touching me.'

'I know,' he muttered. 'That's why I'm letting you go, however painful it is. I can't keep you like a caged bird. You and Josef must make your own——'

His mouth clamped shut and he disappeared under the water in a flurry of spray. Tiffany sat watching where he'd disappeared, her face intent. It was almost as if he was upset.

Her heart thudded and her face cleared, a sudden bright light seeming to illuminate her from within. Hassan *loved* her. Of that she was sure.

She stripped off her clothes. All of them. Somewhere in the darkness, he was swimming, desperately, violently, with a pent-up anger. All that vitality and fierceness, going to waste.

She worked the water into her hair and tried to clean the mud from her skin which felt as if it had been sandpapered. Still Hassan drove himself through the water, backwards and forwards, as if expiating a sin.

'Hassan,' she called. 'Hassan!'

His head bobbed up near her, the water pouring from his ebonised hair, pearlised droplets twinkling on his thick lashes.

'What?' he said ungraciously.

Her mouth curved. She'd seen the raw graze on his neck. There was a way to test her theory.

'You were hurt when the tree crashed into the truck.'

His hand lifted and touched the wound.

'I'll get the sand out,' she offered.

Before he could back away, she had placed her hands on his shoulders and let her fingers drift upwards. Deliberately she ensured that her body should flow against his and he drew in an agonised breath.

'Don't touch me,' he whispered.

Her mouth dropped to his wound and gently licked. A quiver ran through his body and she wrapped her legs around him.

'For God's sake,' he said thickly.

'I don't mind about Abdul,' she said gently, taking his face in her hands. 'I don't mind that you and Faridah were lovers——'

'What?' he exploded.

'I'm sorry,' she said firmly. 'I talked to Faridah. She admitted it all. And I don't mind that you have a son. He'd naturally take first place in your heart. What we both once did is in the past, like Nazim, like everything that's gone between us.'

'Wait a minute,' he said sternly, taking her hands away. 'Faridah is claiming I have a son called Abdul? That he's her son—*our* son?'

'More or less,' she said awkwardly. 'Well, I came to that conclusion and she didn't correct me. You must understand why she told me. She loves you. That's why she hel——' Tiffany broke off, biting her lip.

'I see. She helped you to escape. She poisoned your mind against me.' Hassan's mouth became grim. 'Your trust wasn't very strong, was it? Otherwise why believe her, rather than the evidence of your own eyes, and your instincts?'

'I'd made a mistake before,' she said in a low tone. 'I learnt the painful way not to trust my instincts about men.'

'But it's the only way you can tell,' he said in gentle reproof.

'I almost wanted to believe her,' mused Tiffany. 'Because if I didn't, I'd have to accept that my love for you was as powerful as my love for Jo. I wasn't ready for that, or all of its implications. I didn't want to give up work, to be just your wife, loving you and not being loved in return.'

'Your... love? Did you say...?'

Tiffany held her breath, uncertain that she'd made the right decision. He loves me, he loves me not, he loves me, he loves me not, she chanted to herself, waiting for his reaction.

He didn't give much away. 'Give up work?' he frowned. 'I was expecting you to continue. You're not the kind of woman who enjoys sitting at home. I hadn't planned on your idling away our marriage. Didn't you think you could cope with me and your job?'

There was a faint amusement in his voice, but she had turned away and her face was stony, the terrible disappointment and embarrassment creeping through her. She tried to look aloof and carefree.

'Explain who Abdul al Sharif is,' she demanded. 'I didn't mistake the name. I know there's someone called that,' she persisted stubbornly.

'The only Abdul in our family is hardly a problem where you're concerned,' answered Hassan drily. 'He's my cousin and my closest friend. He runs the New York office for me, controlling those companies I built up there with his help.'

'But I thought...Faridah said...' Tiffany was so appalled by Faridah's duplicity that she found herself under water, and came up spluttering with Hassan's arms holding her securely. He pushed her to the side of the pool where they hauled themselves on to a ledge. His eyes dropped to her breasts as the water streamed from them, and then watched every last drop fall from their hardening points.

'You weren't in love with Faridah?' she asked hopefully.

Hassan was having some difficulty in mastering his self-control and concentrating on her anxious questions.

'Mmm? Of course not! I told you. She loved Nazim. A marriage was arranged between them but he left the country, claiming he wanted to finish his education in England. Once there, he refused to return, or to marry her. It caused a row because father said he had dishonoured her and her family. She came to live with us. We owed it to her. It is now my duty to care for her and protect her because she was wronged by my brother.'

Tiffany felt every bone in her body relax, every muscle, every tight tendon. She smiled blissfully.

'Hassan, I got in a muddle. I overheard you talking about handing over control of companies. I thought you

were hastily getting rid of them to Abdul—your son—
so that Josef couldn't inherit anything.'

'But why would I do that?' he asked in surprise.

'Because Jo had a claim on half of your business,'
she said in a small, apologetic voice. 'He'd take away
some of your power. So I imagined that you meant Josef
harm.'

'Harm? A child?' Hassan looked very hurt. 'My
brother really did sour you against men, didn't he?' he
said quietly. 'Don't worry about the fact that I'm
shedding the US companies. They're but a small section
of the Sharif business. There's more than enough left
for a dozen Josefs, most of them based in Riyam and
Europe. Not too great a commuting distance.'

'Oh, Hassan! You make me sound grabbing! I didn't
mean——!'

'Tiffany, I only wanted to cut down my transatlantic
travel so I could spend all my time with you and Josef.
I'd tied up the New York end rather well, arranging for
Faridah to move there as managing director, under
Abdul—they get on like a house on fire. I intended to
tell her today. She'll do very well. She has a sharp mind.
Too sharp,' he said wryly. 'In fact, your arrival and
Faridah's reaction to you showed me that I was probably
holding her back from marrying. I'd protected her for
too long and she'd become possessive of me. She knows
I don't love her. She's always known that. But she's never
liked me to share my attention, especially with other
women. She leaves in a week. She'll get her marching
orders when I return. I don't think I want anything more
to do with her unless it's absolutely necessary.'

'And you?' asked Tiffany, lifting her body erect.

Hassan was about to turn his head when she caught
his hand and placed it on her heart.

'What do you feel?' she asked softly.

'You must be joking,' he croaked, his thumb jerking away from her nipple.

'The beating of my heart,' she smiled. 'Would it beat hard for a man I hated?'

His glance flicked up to hers.

'I love you,' she said simply, her eyes telling him so.

'After all I've done?' he whispered.

'You wanted to save Jo from a dreadful mother. Then you wanted me——'

'I fell in love,' he corrected, his hand curving around her drum-hard breast. 'Against my will, I fell in love. So crazily that I couldn't think straight, that I wanted you near me every second of the day, breathing the same air.'

She melted towards him. He kissed the line of her hair and slid her into the pool. He moved around her, kissing every inch of her skin where it met the water, working around her body until he had made a complete kissing circle and she was almost climbing up the wall from the erotic experience.

A delicate, wet finger trailed over her full breasts, bringing her nipples into angry, rose-tipped peaks. They submerged. Their bodies slid together, line for line, bone for bone. Her arms floated to his shoulders and then his mouth met hers as their loins jarred together in an unbearable demand.

In a flurry of spray they surfaced, still clinging together. Hassan's eyes were dark and lustrous with passion. Tiffany wound her hands in his thick wet hair and improvised as she'd never done before, wanting desperately to kiss every inch of his face. Then she took the short hairs in front of his ear between her teeth and gently tugged, then licked them flat again.

For the first time in her life, she felt free.

'I've loved you for so long,' she whispered, nibbling his earlobe.

'My darling,' he said, husky with emotion. 'You'll get cold. We must return.'

'You care about me, don't you?'

'Care! Darling, I nearly went mad wondering if I'd reach you before the sandstorm struck. You must have been terrified. Yet you struggled on, for Josef's sake. No mother could have done more to prove what she feels for her son. Come.'

He bundled up their clothes and led her, still naked, up the steps. In the fading warmth of the sun, its red light making their bodies glow, they dried their bodies before dressing each other, tenderly. Then she saw his face darken and become remote.

'What is it?' she asked urgently.

'Faridah,' he snapped. 'I'm thinking what I'll do——'

'No. Think how she must have felt, Hassan!' she cried passionately. 'First she learns that the man she loves has married an English girl. Then that very same woman turns up and appears to be luring away the second man she has fallen for. I don't bear Faridah any malice. I know what it's like to feel jealous and to know a one-sided love.'

'Well, she's going to America sooner than she thinks,' muttered Hassan. 'Would you like us to fly out to Oman, and see Jo? Would you feel safer there?'

'I trust you anywhere,' she smiled, her face radiant.

'Fool,' he laughed, his fingers shaping her waist. 'We'll go and tell your son what we feel about each other.'

'Our son.'

'Our son,' he repeated huskily.

'I'm still your hostage,' she breathed, reaching up and twining her hands around his neck.

'And I am yours,' he said, his lips claiming hers. 'A hostage to love.'

Don't miss one exciting moment of your next vacation with Harlequin's

FREE
FIRST CLASS TRAVEL ALARM CLOCK

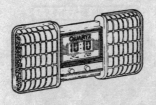

Actual Size
3¼" × 1¼"h

By reading FIRST CLASS—Harlequin Romance's armchair travel plan for the incurably romantic—you'll not only visit a different dreamy destination every month, but you'll also receive a FREE TRAVEL ALARM CLOCK!

All you have to do is collect 2 proofs-of-purchase from FIRST CLASS Harlequin Romance books. FIRST CLASS is a one title per month series, available from January to December 1991.

For further details, see FIRST CLASS premium ads in FIRST CLASS Harlequin Romance books. Look for these books with the special FIRST CLASS cover flash!

JTLOOK-R

Harlequin

HISTORICAL

Christmas

STORIES · 1991

Bring back heartwarming memories of Christmas past
with HISTORICAL CHRISTMAS STORIES 1991,
a collection of romantic stories
by three popular authors.
The perfect Christmas gift!

Don't miss these heartwarming stories,
available in November
wherever Harlequin books are sold:

CHRISTMAS YET TO COME
by Linda Trent
A SEASON OF JOY
by Caryn Cameron
FORTUNE'S GIFT
by DeLoras Scott

**Best Wishes and Season's Greetings
from Harlequin!**

XM-91